DAUGHTER OF TEXAS

TERRI REED

Steeple
Hill®

Published by Steeple Hill Books™

Special thanks and acknowledgment to
Terri Reed for her contribution to the
Texas Ranger Justice miniseries.

STEEPLE HILL BOOKS

Steeple
Hill®

Recycling programs
for this product may
not exist in your area.

ISBN-13: 978-0-373-67446-6

DAUGHTER OF TEXAS

www.SteepleHill.com

Printed in U.S.A.

Delight yourself in the Lord, and He shall give you the desires of your heart.

—*Psalms* 37:4

Writing is never done in a vacuum.
Thank you to my fellow Texas Ranger Justice
authors: Lenora, Valerie, Margaret, Lynette and
Shirlee. You made writing this book fun.
Thank you to Emily Rodmell and the staff at
Steeple Hill Books for coming up with such an
exciting series. And as always, Leah Vale,
Lissa Manley, Melissa McClone and
Ruth Kaufman—I am forever grateful.

ONE

The Ranger creed: "No man in the wrong can stand up against a fellow that's in the right and keeps on a-comin'."

Corinna Pike froze on the unlit front porch of her family's ranch home. Gunfire had come from within the house!

Her startled gaze shot to her father's Crown Victoria parked in the driveway. Her father, the only person she had left in the world, was inside the house.

Terror crashed through her like a runaway freight train.

She exploded into motion, but the front door was locked. She dropped her dance bag, fumbled with her house key, jammed it in the lock and pushed the door open so hard it bounced back from the wall.

"Dad!" she yelled at the top of her lungs.

A chill of dread that had nothing to do with the drop in the late September evening temperature skated across her flesh.

Corinna raced through the darkened hallway of the sprawling, single-story house toward the crack of light coming from beneath her father's study door. As the daughter of a Texas Ranger, running to gunfire was in her blood.

She skidded to a halt and reached for the study's doorknob and flung open the door. The light in the study winked out, throwing the world around her into pitch blackness. A loud feline screech, followed by eighteen pounds of fleeing cat slamming into her legs, made Corinna lurch back.

Before she could even think of shouting out in surprise at her deranged tabby, an explosion of noise erupted. A bright flash of light scalded her eyes. Her ears rang. Something hot sliced across her bare biceps. Searing pain brought tears to her eyes. She'd been shot!

She instinctively dropped to the floor, her hands covering her head. No more bullets came her way. Instead, she heard the patio doors fly open and the sound of running feet leaving the scene.

Around her, the house settled into a stark silence where only the rasp of her own breathing echoed in her ears. The acrid smell of gunpowder permeating the air almost obliterated the coppery scent of blood assaulting her senses.

The moon's light spilled into the study through the open patio doors outlining the desk. Staying low, she edged along the wall toward it. Using the desk as cover, she reached for the lamp with her right hand and winced with pain at the effort to raise her injured arm. Switching to her uninjured arm, she flipped the control knob. Soft light made her blink as she adjusted to the brightness. Cautiously, she peered out into the room.

She didn't see anyone ready to take another shot at her, but the sight before her was even more horrifying.

Her gaze landed on her father sprawled across the thick wool rug in front of his cherrywood desk. Everything inside her recoiled. Her mind tried to process what she saw, her feet felt rooted in place.

Her father's service weapon lay beside him. Blood oozed from a gunshot wound in his chest just below the Texas Ranger badge pinned to his plaid flannel shirt, soaking the beige carpet beneath him a deep crimson red.

Her wild gaze swept the room again looking for a threat and landed on an unfamiliar man's prone body. He had a similar wound in his abdomen.

The man, mid-thirties and looking very much out of place with his dirty clothes and matted dark hair, lay very still.

She didn't see a weapon in his hand.

Crying out in anguish, Corinna crawled as best she could with one arm to her father's side. "Please, don't let him be dead."

A high keening noise filled the room. Vaguely aware the sound came from her, she reached a shaky hand to his neck and pressed her fingers to the spot where a pulse should beat. Nothing.

Agony trapped her breath in her lungs. She fell forward, her head coming to rest on her father's broad shoulder. First her mother, now her father. The two people she loved most in the world both taken from her. Her mother by sickness, her father…murdered.

How could God let this happen?

Forcing herself to move, to assess the situation, she asked herself, What would her father do?

She scrambled over to the other man and checked for a pulse. Beneath her fingers she felt the faint beat of his heart.

Quickly, and without regard to her own pain, she ripped off her navy sweatshirt with the orange-and-white roadrunner logo of the University of Texas, San Antonio. She pressed the wadded-up material against the man's wound to stem the flow of blood seeping from his abdomen.

She needed help. She ran to the credenza and grabbed the cordless phone with the hand of her uninjured side.

A cat yowled to her left.

Corinna jumped at Gabby's unexpected cry, her heart still racing from being shot at, her breath stalled in her chest. The orange tabby stood on the threshold of the open double French doors leading to the back patio. Corinna breathed a sigh of relief. If it hadn't been for Gabby's forceful exit just minutes ago, Corinna might be dead.

In the distance the sound of an engine turned over, roared and then faded away. The killer getting away. Returning to the stranger's side to press the hand of her wounded arm on the bunched-up sweatshirt, she dialed 911 with her other hand. Her gaze shifted back to her father.

A sob caught in her throat. Now she was truly alone in the world.

Texas Ranger Ben Fritz threw his Jeep into park on the curving, graveled driveway of the ranch behind the small compact car belonging to Corinna, Captain Pike's daughter.

Gut churning, Ben glanced once more at the

cryptic text message he'd received on his cell phone from his boss, Texas Ranger Captain Gregory Pike, only twenty minutes ago.

CONVENE AT MY HOUSE, ASAP. MAJOR CASE ABOUT TO EXPLODE.

What was Greg working on that was so volatile?

No way would he call the Rangers to his house for a case with his adult daughter in attendance. Greg had kept his private life as isolated from his job as possible.

When he'd first received the text, Ben had been bothered that Greg had kept a case from him. But his annoyance evaporated. Something weird was going on and Greg had reached out to him. Apprehension slithered down Ben's spine like a rattler on the loose as he jumped out of his Jeep.

Lights from the cars of other Rangers, the elite law enforcement agency unique to Texas, cut through the twilight, illuminating the front of the Pike house, an expansive L-shaped place set back from the road. The circular driveway wrapped around a grassy area with a magnolia tree, a cedar bench, and a few small bushes that would flower in the spring.

Obviously, all the Rangers of Company D had received Greg's text. This was serious.

Oliver Drew climbed out of his 4x4, the red paint barely visible beneath a thick layer of grime and dust. Ben paused to wait for the half Native-American Ranger. He sported his usual leather vest over a long-sleeve white button-down, jeans and scuffed boots.

Tall, well-built and oozing with charm, Daniel Boone Riley adjusted his standard issue white cowboy hat over his dark hair as he stepped from his truck. His eyes were troubled as they met Ben's gaze.

More vehicles barreled down the drive and halted, stacked end to end like slot cars ready for the races. Cade Jarvis, Trevor Donovan, Marvel Jones, Levi McDonnell and Gisella Hernandez, the lone female of their company, got out of their vehicles and joined Ben. Only two were missing, Anderson Michaels and Evan Chen. Evan was on assignment over in Corpus Christie and would no doubt check in. And Ben knew Anderson would arrive as soon as possible from wherever he was.

It was the Ranger way to drop whatever they were doing to answer the call. Ben had been grocery shopping. He'd abandoned his cart in the middle of the produce aisle.

"Any idea what this is about?" Oliver asked.

"None." Ben started toward the front porch.

"What case was the captain working?" asked Gisella, falling in step behind Ben.

"Don't know," Daniel replied.

Ben stopped in his tracks. Since the porch light wasn't on, he hadn't noticed that the front door stood wide open. The hairs on the back of his neck rose in alert. He held up a hand to halt his fellow Rangers. He pointed at the open door.

Cade tapped Levi on the shoulder. "We'll take the back," Cade said in a low voice as he unholstered his weapon from his belt.

The wail of a siren punctuated the air, intensifying the unease gripping Ben. He motioned for the others to follow as he drew his sidearm. They entered the house in standard two-by-two formation. Ben directed Gisella and Oliver to peel off toward the unlit living room, while he motioned for Daniel and Marvel to head down the darkened hall toward the bedrooms. Then Ben, with Trevor at his back, moved toward the only lit room. Greg's study.

The scene that met them rocked Ben back on

his heels. Horror filled his senses as he tried to process what he was seeing.

Greg, his mentor and friend, lay on the floor. Blood pooled around him. Another man, also shot, was sprawled a few feet away. Greg's daughter, dressed in loose sweatpants and a pale purple leotard covered in blood, sat beside the man, her knees drawn to her chest, her head bowed so that only one side of her pale face was visible. One hand pressed a wad of material to his wound. A black cordless phone dangled from the other.

Acting on instinct and training, Ben quickly searched for the unidentified man's weapon. And found none. Pulling a handkerchief from his pocket, Ben picked up Greg's weapon and sniffed the end. He frowned. The gun hadn't been fired recently.

Obviously, this wasn't a Western-style shootout. Whoever had fired the fatal shots was gone, along with the murder weapon.

Cade and Levi entered through the open patio doors. A hiss of surprise came from Gisella as she stepped up behind Ben. More shocked exclamations followed as the Rangers slipped carefully into the room.

Ben went to Greg and squatted down to check

his pulse. Grief sucked the air from his body. He looked at his comrades and shook his head.

"This one's still breathing," Cade said as he checked the pulse of the other man.

Ben shoved his own anguish aside to be dealt with later and focused on Corinna. By profession, Corinna was a prima ballerina with the San Antonio Ballet Company, like her mother before her. Amanda Pike had died of breast cancer when Corinna was young, not long before Ben had met Greg.

He moved closer and touched her shoulder. She flinched. A knot formed in his gut. She looked so small and vulnerable.

Had she witnessed her father's murder? Fresh sorrow and compassion tightened his chest. Protective instincts rose despite the antagonism that had always sparked between them. He wanted to shield this fragile ballerina from the harsh reality of her father's death.

The sound of booted feet brought Ben's gaze around. Sheriff Karl Layton, a tall man with shocking white hair and chiseled features pushed his way into the room. Layton inclined his head, his question clear. *Was Pike alive?*

Ben shook his head as another wave of grief flowed through him. Layton blew out a breath and tears misted the older man's eyes. Greg and Karl had been close friends from way back.

Layton swiped a hand over his face. "Dispatch relayed the 911 call."

The sound of an ambulance arriving let Ben know they only had a few minutes to collect information before the body was remanded to the local police force. His gut twisted with grief. Greg wasn't just any body. He'd been a father figure to Ben for more than a decade.

Shifting his focus from Greg, Ben said to his men, "Work the scene. Get the SAPD crime response unit in here pronto while the evidence is still fresh."

"Already made the call," Cade replied, his normally tanned skin ashen.

Gently, Ben took the phone from Corinna's hand and passed it to Oliver. Her skin was pasty white; her dark hair had loosened from her normally severe bun. And her dark eyes were glassy as she stared off into space. Taking Corinna's shoulders in his hands, he pulled her to her feet. She didn't resist. Ben figured shock was setting in.

When she turned to face toward him, his heart contracted painfully in his chest. "You're hurt!"

She didn't seem to hear him.

Blood seeped from a scrape on her right upper biceps. He inspected the wound. Looked like a bullet had grazed her. Whoever had killed her father had tried to kill her. With aching ferocity, rage roared through Ben. "Get the paramedics."

"On it." Cade pivoted to disappear out the door. A moment later, he returned with one of the emergency personnel in tow while the rest rushed by to help the injured man.

"Excuse me, sir," the young blond man said to Ben. "Let me take a look at her injury."

Ben stepped back but held firmly to her slender hand.

"It's a surface wound that will probably leave a small scar," the paramedic stated as he placed a bandage over the gash. "The heat of the bullet cauterized the flesh. It will heal quickly enough."

But Ben had a feeling that her heart wouldn't heal anytime soon. She'd adored her father. That had been apparent from the moment Ben stepped foot into the Pike world. She'd barely tolerated Ben from the get-go with her icy stares and brusque manner, making it clear she thought him not good enough to be in her world. But when it came to her father...

Greg had known that if anything happened to

him, she'd need help coping with the loss and ensuing devastation.

"Ben, I need you to promise me if anything ever happens to me, you'll watch out for Corinna. She'll need an anchor. I fear she's too fragile to suffer another death."

Of course Ben had promised. Though he'd refused to even allow the thought that any harm would befall his mentor and friend to form. He'd wanted to believe Greg was indestructible. But he wasn't. None of them were.

The Rangers were human and very mortal, performing a risky job that put their lives on the line every day.

Never before had Ben been so acutely aware of that fact.

Now his captain was gone. It was up to him to not only bring Greg's murderer to justice, but to protect and help Corinna.

Tucking her small frame against his side, he led her away from the scene of the crime and into the living room. He flipped on the table lamp before guiding Corinna to the worn navy blue leather couch.

She'd been a gawky pre-teen with a mouth full of braces and an attitude of superiority that had grated on Ben when he'd first met her. He'd watched her transform into a Texas Rose—beautiful, poised, aloof and way off-limits.

At least for a guy like him.

Now Corinna was an orphan. Something they had in common. His heart twisted with empathy and remembered pain. All the confusion, anguish and utter helplessness of losing his parents still swirled around his heart, even after more than two decades.

Ben gathered Corinna's hands in his. He'd walk through this with her every step of the way. But first he had to know what had happened. "Corinna, I need you to talk to me."

Her lips trembled but no words came. Large tears slid from her eyes to mingle with the blood on her cheek. It hurt him to see her so distraught.

"Can you tell me what happened?" he asked.

She blinked, a slow sweep of long dark lashes. Turning her head to meet his gaze, she said in a soft, broken voice, "Someone killed him."

"Did you see who shot your father?"

She shook her head. "I heard the gunfire as I arrived."

He hated to push Corinna for fear she might break, but he needed to know what she'd seen so they could follow the fresh trail to Greg's killer.

"I need you to walk me through this. You arrived and heard the gun. Were you in your car?"

She shook her head. "On the porch."

"How many shots did you hear?"

"Two."

He rubbed her arms, careful not to go near the stark white bandage wrapped around her biceps. "Okay. That's good. You heard two shots. Then what happened? Did someone run out?"

"No. I ran in. The study light was on. Then it wasn't. I—" She closed her eyes.

He sensed she was close to the edge, but he had to know. "You what?"

"I opened the door."

"What did you see?"

She began to rock slightly, back and forth. Back and forth. "Nothing. Gabby startled me and I jerked back." She lifted her gaze, her obsidian eyes filled with horror. "Someone shot at me."

"Did you see anyone?"

"Too dark. I hid. The person ran out through the patio doors."

Grateful that she'd had the presence of mind to hide, he asked, "When you turned the light on, was...your dad like you found him?"

"Yes. But…he wasn't breathing." Her voice broke on a sob.

"Do you know the other man? Do you know why he was with your father?"

"No. No, I don't."

"Did you hear anything else? Voices? See anyone?"

She shifted her gaze away toward the window. "I heard the distant sound of an engine."

Ben glanced out the picture window at the back of the living room to the acreage where he knew a dozen or so horses grazed. The killer could have used the property's rear gate.

"We should question the neighboring ranchers. See if anyone saw a vehicle leaving the premises," Trevor stated in his brusque manner. "Cade, Levi, go."

The two agents looked to Ben for confirmation. Ben nodded. "And check the gate. That could have been the escape route."

The two men hustled out of the house. Ben noted Trevor's frown but now was not the time to deal with the pecking order within the Rangers.

He refocused on Corinna. "Do you normally arrive home at this time?"

"No. I'm usually much later, but Kyle's sick.

Hard to practice the duet routines without him," she said.

Was it coincidence that her dance partner had been sick or a ruse to get her home? Was she the intended target? Ben knew of Kyle Dennison, though they'd never met. He would run a check on Dennison as a precaution. At this point, he couldn't overlook anyone as a potential suspect.

Anything out of the ordinary required examination. They didn't know what or who they were dealing with.

If only Greg had kept Ben in the loop on what he'd been working on before it became a dire situation. If only he'd contacted Ben sooner…

Oliver stepped forward, his dark eyes on Corinna. "So you heard nothing that would tell us who did this?"

"No. Just the gun…" A sob broke from her and she buried her face in her hands.

Ben gathered her stiff form close, letting her cry. He hadn't had much opportunity to comfort grieving women. Doing so felt awkward and yet, tenderness rose to the surface, making him tighten his arms around her. She felt so delicate and defenseless in his arms.

The white bandage covering her biceps glowed like a neon sign. A few more inches and the bullet could have lodged in her heart. She'd come close to dying tonight.

Just like her father. Grief battled to be loosened. He held it in check. This was not the time to give vent to his emotions. He had to stay focused. Greg would have counted on Ben to find his murderer. As well as protect Corinna. Failure at either task was not an option, which only served to increase the pressure building in Ben's chest.

Corinna clutched the front of his chambray shirt. A haunted look darkened her eyes. "You have to find the person who did this."

"I will," he vowed as he pulled her back to his chest.

No matter what it took, he would bring down Captain Pike's murderer. For Corinna. For all of them.

TWO

Ben's strong arms encircled Corinna, buffeting her from the raging nightmare going on around her as uniformed San Antonio police officers filled her house. She shifted on the couch. Biting pain from the wound on her arm zinged through her. Never in a million years would she have thought she'd be in this position.

Acutely aware of Ben's closeness, she allowed him to hold her, needing his strength. At the moment, she had none of her own.

His heart pounded like thunder in her ears through his shirt, drowning out the crackle of radios and dismay of law enforcement officers as they discovered one of their own had been murdered. The cotton fabric of Ben's shirt, so soft against her cheek, smelled freshly laundered. She focused on the little things. That's all she could do right now.

She squeezed her eyes tight.

Why couldn't this be a nightmare? Why couldn't she open her eyes and find herself back at the dance studio? Or better yet, back to this morning when she'd kissed her father goodbye for the day, not realizing it would be the last time she'd ever see him alive.

A sob of pain and grief lodged in her throat. Tears leaked from her closed eyes. She fought to hold them back. She was usually so good at keeping her emotions under control.

But the image of her father lying in a pool of his own blood blazed in her head, forever imprinted in her mind. She shuddered. Ben's hands smoothed over her back in a calming rhythm. He would find whoever had done this. Her father had trusted Ben.

Truth be told, so did she, even if she did harbor anger and resentment toward Ben for invading their lives and taking her father's attention away from her. Every time they went off to do "guy" things, Corinna had seethed inside and longed to be included. She never was. They had locked her out of that world. Though as she'd grown older she'd resigned herself to being excluded, she still blamed the man her father had taken under his wing. The son he'd never had.

"Ben, we need you in here," said a deep voice that Corinna recognized as Ranger Marvel Jones. He was a tall African-American man with a shaved head.

She felt Ben nod.

"In a minute," Ben replied. "Can you ask Gisella to come here?"

"Sure thing," Marvel said.

Ben tried to ease Corinna out of his arms. She resisted, unwilling to face reality on her own. Here, within Ben's embrace, she felt safe, felt protected from the grief waiting to overwhelm her.

It didn't make sense. He was the last person in the world she should be looking to for solace. Old wounds full of antagonism stirred, but the overpowering anguish wouldn't let anything else in.

"Corinna, honey, I need to talk to you. Please, look at me," Ben said, his voice soft and coaxing.

She shook her head. "I can't," she whispered, not wanting to break the protective barrier of isolation that kept reality at bay. She squeezed her grip on his shirt, pulling herself tighter against his chest.

With gentle yet firm pressure he pushed her

away and lifted her chin with the tips of his fingers. "Open your eyes."

Reluctantly, she did as he asked. For a moment her eyes wouldn't focus, but then his familiar and handsome face came into view.

She stared at him dispassionately and took in his features, the strong jaw, lean cheekbones, straight nose. She liked the way his warm brown, close-cropped hair spiked up in front, giving him a roguish appeal. His dark brown eyebrows slashed over hazel eyes.

Eyes so full of the same pain and grief she felt.

Fresh tears burned the back of her eyes. Tears for this man whom her father had loved like a son. Ben was grieving, too.

From the moment her father had brought him home when he was a teenager, he'd been her rival for her father's attention. He'd won.

Ben had become the son her father had wanted. The one he'd confided in, the one he took to his favorite sports events, the one who'd been groomed to follow in her father's footsteps.

Oh, she'd never doubted her father's love for her. He'd always attend her recitals, made a big deal of her birthdays and lavished her with gifts at Christmas, but it wasn't the same as wanting to be with her.

An intense pain, a familiar ache of losing a parent—losing the person who knew, supported and loved you no matter what—lanced through her. Her chest tightened. Daddy. She would give up everything to have him back with her even for just a moment so she could tell him she loved him. But that would never happen.

Neither she nor Ben had had a chance to say goodbye.

"You got here before the police," Corinna said aloud, realizing that several Rangers had arrived before she'd even heard the sirens.

He nodded. "Yes. The captain sent out a message to come here."

Her pulse spiked. "He needed you."

Guilt flashed across his face. "Yes. If only I'd been closer, arrived sooner, maybe I could have prevented his murder."

She wanted to blame him. To shout that *yes, he should have been here to stop this from happening,* but deep inside she knew that wasn't fair. "If you had been here, you probably would have been shot as well." She swallowed back the bile that rose. "If I had come home any earlier…" Her voice trailed off as the thought played itself out in her head. If she'd arrived any earlier, she, too, could very well be dead right now, not just injured.

Ben took in a sharp breath. "Thankfully, you didn't." He eased apart from her and stood. "I need to talk with Gisella for a moment."

Her gaze slid to the female Ranger standing in the doorway, patiently awaiting Ben. Pallor underscored her olive skin and her dark eyes were sad. Dressed in worn blue jeans, soft leather boots and a Western-cut pale blue blouse, she didn't look like a Ranger. Corinna wondered fleetingly what she did when not on duty.

"I'll be right back," Ben said and walked away.

Wrapping her arms around her middle, Corinna kept her gaze trained on Ben as he stood quietly talking with Gisella. From her peripheral vision she saw the EMTs roll in a gurney. Deep inside she knew it wasn't for her father. Her father was dead. He'd be leaving with the coroner.

No, the gurney was for the man who'd survived the attack.

The man who might know who killed her father.

After a few moments, Ben and Gisella walked over to the couch, blocking Corinna's view as the unidentified man was wheeled out. She dropped her gaze to her clenched hands. Her mind replayed the last images she had of her father. His body sprawled across the floor, blood staining the shirt she'd ironed for him that morning. His dear face frozen in death. A shudder ripped through her.

Gisella remained standing while Ben sat beside Corinna on the couch, crowding her space. His big, strong hands engulfed her slender, delicate ones, making her feel so small and helpless. She didn't like the feeling at all, but at the moment, didn't have the power to fight against it.

"You can't stay here," Ben said.

"Do you really think the person who shot at me might come back?"

"I don't want to take any chances," he said. "He can't know for sure you didn't see him."

She hated the thought of being run out of her house. She wished she could be strong enough to stay. But…not tonight. Her father had been killed here. His blood still stained the carpet. Her blood was splattered on the door. She wondered if she'd ever be able to enter the study again.

Grief twisted her insides, making her ache way worse than any wound to her arm could. "There's living quarters in the barn out back. I'll stay there."

From the way his lips flattened into a grim line, she could tell he wasn't hip to her plan. "It would be better if you stayed somewhere else. Gisella has offered her house."

"No. I wouldn't want to bother anyone, even another Ranger." Just the thought of the sympathy and hovering that her friends would do, made her recoil. She didn't like to be coddled. She straightened her shoulders. "I'm staying. This is my home. I'll not be run off. Someone needs to tend to the animals. Besides, how would anyone know I was in the barn?"

Disapproval flashed in his eyes. "I don't think this is a good idea."

"Not your call, Ben."

His mouth pressed into a grim line. "Then I'll have SAPD post a guard outside."

"Fine." She appreciated his concern and caution, though she doubted it would be needed. "I'll need to pack a few things to take out there with me."

He pulled her to her feet and walked her toward her room, keeping his body between her line of vision and the study. Once they reached her room, he backed away with a nod, his face grim.

Gisella stepped into the room. "What can I do to help?"

Bring my father back to life. The thought flittered across Corinna's mind. But no one could do that.

Her hands curled into fists. Anger roared through her like a lion on the chase.

Her soul cried out to God, *Why? Why did You let him die, too?*

Her faith in God had been rocked when her mother had died. She hadn't understood why God had allowed the sickness to overtake her. Why, if God was the great physician, hadn't He answered her prayers and healed her?

Her father had assured her God did love her. That God was good. That sickness was a part of the human condition. Words that didn't offer comfort to a twelve-year-old girl.

Her father had also told her to remember she'd see her mother again one day in Heaven. Corinna had clung to that thought. And as long as God kept her father safe, she could cling to Him, too.

But now her father was dead.

God had turned His back on her prayers. God had never loved her. She didn't even know if there really was a Heaven. She had nothing to cling to anymore. Her faith had been shaken to the core.

* * *

The barn's living quarters consisted of a loft space with a pullout sleeper sofa, TV, table and chair. Ben had stayed in the loft on numerous occasions when he'd first met Greg and had needed a place to stay until he could afford his apartment. A small refrigerator sat in one corner and a wood stove with a pipe chimney took up space in the middle of the loft.

As Ben lit the stove to warm up the loft, he said, "I really wish you'd reconsider staying here."

She arched an eyebrow at him. He figured she was going for haughty, but all he saw was a woman close to the breaking point.

"This is my home. My life. I get to decide. I can understand your concern, really, I can. But you've taken precautions. There isn't anything more you can do."

Even though he'd made arrangements to have a guard posted on the property, he had a bad feeling about leaving Corinna here. He couldn't take chances with Greg's daughter's life. She was his responsibility now. He would protect her, be there for her and guide her as best he could.

As best she'd let him.

He didn't doubt that once the shock wore off,

Corinna's icy superiority would return to replace the vulnerability in her pretty eyes.

And short of hauling her in for some trumped-up charge, he really had no say in where she stayed.

Before leaving, he made sure she had her cell phone and his number on speed dial in case of an emergency.

"I'll be fine." She'd moved to stand at the top of the loft stairs, her arms crossed over her chest, looking as if she were trying to contain her grief. "You go do what you need to do to find my father's killer and don't worry about me."

Easier said than accomplished. But he left her in the barn and headed to the house. Back inside the study, Ben's gaze fell on the dark crimson spot tarnishing the thick rug.

Both Greg and the other man were gone. Greg to the morgue, the mystery guy to the hospital with Marvel and Daniel riding along. The two Rangers had instructions to stick close to the man in case he awoke and also to provide protection.

Ben didn't want the assassin trying to finish the job before they could get information out of the man who might hold the key to Greg's murder.

Ranger Anderson Michaels stepped to Ben's side, his thunderous expression reflecting the rage gathering steam inside Ben. "No weapon. No fingerprints, no shoe prints outside, either."

Ben grunted in response. "A professional hit. Do you know what case Greg was working?"

"No. Care to enlighten me?"

"Seems he didn't share it with any of us. Must have been a new case."

Anderson gave him a quick glance. "You didn't know? That's so...wrong."

Ben shrugged back the hurt trying to worm its way into his consciousness.

"Yes, it's wrong," Trevor remarked as he joined them just inside the doorway of the study. Tall and lanky with blond hair graying at the temples, his blue eyes were hard as ice. "The captain should've kept us in the loop. He was too much of a one-man show."

Ben fisted his hands and slowly turned to face Trevor. "Do not ever besmirch the captain again."

Trevor held up his hands, palms facing out. "Hey, I'm just telling it like it is. Pike was a good captain, but he kept too much too close to the vest. We're a team, remember?"

"Yeah, I remember." Ben rolled the tension from his shoulders as he tried not to see the truth in Trevor's words. Greg had kept information from the team on occasion.

One incident in particular came to mind. There had been a string of jewelry store heists across the state. Somehow, Greg had had a lead on one of the thieves. He'd staked out the guy's house. Alone.

He'd captured the man and then called in the bust. A stash of jewels had been found on the premises and the thief turned on his cohorts.

The situation had ended well. But it could have gone terribly wrong. Greg had gone against protocol, risking his life and the investigation. His defense was that he'd worked alone to minimize the chances the guy would get spooked and flee.

This time, Greg's holding back had cost him his life.

"I want a thorough search of the house," Ben said, loud enough for them all to hear. "There has to be some clue as to why Greg was killed."

"On it," Anderson said and moved away.

Ben didn't have to give further instruction. The team knew what to do.

Ben ignored Trevor's sharp glance. Though they shared the rank of lieutenant, Trevor had transferred over from Company A last year, so he was fairly new to the team. He hadn't been with the company nearly as long as Ben and, therefore, hadn't earned the respect and loyalty needed to lead the team. Having a short temper hadn't won him any points, either. Ben wondered if the man was as tightly wound with his wife and daughters as he was with his comrades.

Ben had met Trevor's wife, Sarah Donovan, once, at the Christmas party last year. A quiet, pretty lady who had seemed to prefer to stay in the background than have attention centered on her. Ben had liked her. The verdict was still out on Trevor.

Several hours later, their search of the house hadn't revealed anything. Still no closer to knowing what was going on, Ben left the crime scene techs to finish up at the Pike home and secured an SAPD officer to stand watch near the barn.

Ben headed to the hospital. Hopefully, their mysterious victim had awoken and could shed some light on the night's events. He drove through the quiet streets of San Antonio, noting that on this late September night there was little traffic and the hospital parking lot was nearly empty.

After stopping by the administration desk where he was given directions, Ben made his way to the fourth floor. Daniel and Marvel stood guard in front of the closed door of their victim's room.

"Hey, Ben," Daniel greeted him.

"Has he awakened?" Ben asked.

Daniel's eyes looked troubled. "No. Doc says the guy's in a coma. He can't predict when or if he'll come out of it."

Not the news Ben wanted to hear. Disappointment fed his anger. "I'll contact SAPD and get around-the-clock guards on this guy. Until then, you two okay to stay?"

Marvel nodded. "I don't have anyone waiting at home for me, so yeah, I can stay."

"No hot dates tonight?" Daniel teased.

Marvel grinned, even white teeth flashing against his chocolate skin. "Nope. Free agent these days. But I do have my eye on a little filly I met in the park."

Marvel was a real ladies' man, but so far no woman had captured the marathon runner's heart. "How about you, Daniel? You good to stay the night?"

Daniel shrugged. "Whatever it takes."

Ben nodded, knowing he could always count on the Ranger. Daniel came from wealth but chose to live a life dedicated to serving justice. A life that sometimes came with a price. For Daniel, that had been the loss of his marriage and estrangement from his son.

"When the uniforms show, you're free to leave. We'll convene in the morning at the office." Ben pressed his lips together as a wave of sorrow hit. He wouldn't be seeing Greg tomorrow. Not ever again.

Daniel put his hand on Ben's shoulder. "We'll find the guy who did this."

Ben wished he had the same confidence echoing in Daniel's voice. He cleared his throat, forcing back his emotions. "Yeah. Call if anything develops."

The sound of rubber-soled shoes on linoleum disturbed the quiet hallway. Ben turned to see a white-coated man in his mid-thirties approaching.

"Doctor Vargas," Daniel said below his breath.

Ben stepped forward. The doctor came to a stop.

"Gentlemen, I see you're still here," the doctor said in a thick Spanish accent.

Ben stuck out his hand. "Ranger Fritz."

"Doctor Ramon Vargas." They shook hands.

"We'll be arranging an around-the-clock guard detail for the man in this room," Ben said.

The doctor's dark eyebrows rose. "I thought he was a victim, not a criminal."

"We don't know what he is at this point. And until he wakes up, we're sticking close." Ben glanced at the door. "I'd like to see him."

"I'm sure you're aware he's unconscious," the doctor stated with a slight rebuff in his tone.

"I understand," Ben said, his voice mild, but he held the man's gaze, making it clear he'd have his way.

Doctor Vargas inclined his head. "Of course. Always willing to cooperate with the authorities."

Something in the doctor's voice snagged Ben's attention. But the congenial expression on the man's face belied any antagonism. Shrugging it off as trauma from the night's events, Ben entered the hospital room.

The man lying on the bed was a Caucasian male, with shaggy black hair, pale skin. He looked to be about five foot ten in height with an average build. There was a slight scar under his left eye. No tattoos on his arms, which rested on the blanket covering his body. IVs and monitors were hooked up to the guy. He looked like he was peacefully sleeping.

Somewhere Ben had heard that people in comas could hear what was going on around them. Maybe he'd wake up if Ben talked to him. It was worth a shot.

Because at the moment, this man was the key to finding Corinna's father's murderer.

Ben moved to stand next to the bed and leaned in close. "I don't know if you can hear me or not. My name's Ben Fritz. I'm with the Texas Rangers. You should wake up now and tell us what happened."

Ben waited. The man didn't stir. Disappointment spiraled through him. Maybe it was too soon.

"I told you he was unconscious," Doctor Vargas said from the foot of the bed.

"So you did. Any idea when he'll wake up?"

The doctor gave him a droll look. "I'm not a psychic, Ranger Fritz. When his mind and body are ready to heal, they will."

Ben nodded. "I pray it's sooner rather than later."

The doctor inclined his head and left the room. Ben followed him out.

"Keep me posted," he said to Daniel and Marvel before leaving the hospital.

Fifteen minutes later Ben arrived at his apartment complex outside downtown San Antonio in the northern suburb of Hollywood Park. His one-bedroom apartment was on the second floor in the back overlooking the pool and hot tub. On cool evenings like this it was quiet, but in the summers, when the children were out of school, the noise level rose to deafening decibels. Ben didn't mind.

He rather liked the sound of kids having fun as they played in the curved swimming pool and visited in the common area. Happy noises that stirred hope of one day having a family, a wife and children of his own. His dismal upbringing— orphaned by the drug trade at five and then bouncing around foster homes—could have squashed that dream, not to mention his occupation…but the hope of a family of his own still thrived.

Tonight, only the gurgle of the hot tub floated on the cool air as he made his way up the stairs. He entered his dark apartment and went to his bedroom to sit on the edge of the double bed. His numbed feelings slowly gave way to the grief and anguish of finding his captain murdered. Ben slipped from the bed to land on his knees.

Welling grief, sorrow and anger expanded in his chest until he thought he might explode. Silent sobs wracked his body. His heart throbbed with pain.

"I don't understand, Lord. Why did this happen?"

Silence met his cry.

Ben dropped his face into his hands and wept for the man who had been the closest thing to a real, loving father that Ben had ever known. Greg had taken the time to teach Ben not only about law enforcement, specifically being a Ranger, but had taught him how to be a man. To be kind and fair yet never back down from the principles that they lived by. Greg had included Ben in his and Corinna's family circle, small as it was.

He'd enjoyed and looked forward to many holidays spent together at the Pike house. Memories flittered across Ben's mind. Though they'd exchanged gifts every year, for Ben the best gift of all had been the time spent with the Pikes. Though he and Corinna hadn't had much of a relationship—she'd always been cool and aloof—he'd still enjoyed seeing her joy at the gifts her father abundantly gave her.

Fresh tears spilled down his cheeks.

Holidays wouldn't be the same. He didn't know

if Corinna would want to spend them with him. He doubted so since it would just be the two of them now. They didn't know each other well. She barely tolerated him as it was. A hollow feeling filled the pit of his stomach.

He didn't know how he was going to be able to keep his promise to Greg. He could only hope God would provide the way.

His cell rang, the shrill sound startling in the quiet. Hoping the call was a break in the case, Ben scrambled to pluck the device from the top of the dresser.

He pulled himself together and managed to answer without sounding like he'd been blubbering like a baby. "Fritz."

"Hi, it's me, Corinna." Her soft, feminine voice sounded a bit shaky.

Concern flared. "Are you okay?"

"I'm…coping. You?"

He relaxed, letting the tension in his shoulders ease. "Coping is a good way to describe it."

"How is the other vic…victim?"

His heart twisted to hear the catch in her voice. "He's in a coma. I have guards posted outside his room."

"You really think the killer will come after him again?"

"I do. I just pray he awakens soon and can tell us who we're looking for."

"I hope that, too. This whole night seems so surreal."

Ben understood. He could only imagine how devastated she must be. Greg had always said Corinna was the ray of sunshine that made his world brighter even during the darkest cases. Ben's chest squeezed. Who would Corinna bring sunshine to now?

Forcing himself to speak past the tightness constricting his throat, he said, "If you need anything, Corinna, you can count on all of the Rangers. We are your family now."

A moment of silence filled the line. "Thank you. I'll say good night now."

"Good night."

There'd been an undertone in her voice. Something different than he'd ever heard before. Anger? Hurt?

He smacked his head. She'd just lost her father. Of course she was hurting. They both were.

He vowed to do whatever it took to make the person responsible for their pain pay. Dearly.

THREE

Corinna stared at the bright blue numbers on the clock. 3:00 a.m. She couldn't sleep. The nocturnal noises of the horses and other animals that made the barn their home kept her nerves stretched taut. Finally, she left the warmth of the pullout sofa and padded barefoot across the wood plank floor to the refrigerator hoping to find something inside to drink. She wasn't really surprised to see the fridge empty. It had been a long time since anyone had stayed in the loft.

Maybe the officer outside would be willing to go inside and retrieve some snacks for her.

Slipping on her fuzzy blue slippers and feeling the weight of her "just in case" gun deep in the folds of one robe pocket and her cell phone in the other, she left the loft and made her way outside into the yard lit by the glow of a full moon. Gabby followed closely at her heels. Corinna didn't see her guard. He must be positioned in a strategic place somewhere in the front of the house. She wished she'd thought to ask for his name so she could call out to him.

At the sliding glass door to the dining room, she hesitated. Ben had made it clear the house was an active crime scene and she wasn't to go back inside.

But the crime had happened in the study, not the kitchen.

And she had no intention of going anywhere near where her father had died.

With resolve that she'd apologize later if need be, she entered the dining room, and Gabby darted past her into the dark house. Corinna hurried straight to the refrigerator. Since she was there, she decided to grab a bag of potato chips, her one junk food vice, as well as a carton of orange juice.

A noise disturbed the quiet of the house. Corinna jerked, nearly dropping the bag of chips even as her mind reassured her the noise was just her cat, Gabby.

Suddenly, she desperately wished she'd listened to Ben and gone to stay somewhere else.

But her father raised her not to be a coward.

She needed to stand on her own two feet.

Which meant facing things that went bump in the night. Especially when it was just her cat getting into who knew what.

She left her goodies on the kitchen counter and stepped toward the dark hall. "Gabby?"

A scraping sound came from behind the yellow-taped off, closed door of her father's study. How had the cat found her way in there? Blood pounded in her ears. The last time she'd opened these doors, she'd been shot and then she'd found her father dead on the floor.

Refusing to allow the memories to paralyze her, she rushed out of the house the way she'd come in and hurried toward the patio doors. She skidded to a halt. The doors stood wide open. Corinna swallowed back her rising fear as she took out her cell and called Ben.

A man dressed in all black stepped out of the study onto the patio. Corinna screamed, hoping to alert the officer out front, and jammed her free hand into her pocket. The intruder turned toward her, his face awash in the moonlight. When he started toward her, she wrestled her weapon free, took aim and fired.

The shrill ring of a phone jolted Ben to consciousness from a troubled sleep. He still had difficulty coming to grips with the reality that Greg was gone. The ringing continued.

He jerked upright, his eyes quickly adjusting to his shadowy bedroom. The noise emanated from his lit-up cell on top of his dresser where he'd left it before climbing exhausted into bed. A quick glance at the red numbers on his bedside clock revealed the time, three-thirty in the morning.

That got his blood pumping. He flung the covers aside and reached the dresser in two long strides. He palmed the phone and checked the caller ID.

The call was coming from Corinna's phone.

His heart slammed against his ribs. He pressed the talk button. "Corinna?"

"Come quick," she said in a shaky voice. "I need you. Hey!"

The line went dead.

"Corinna!" he shouted into the silence.

She was in danger! Something had happened.

Pulse-pounding dread filled his veins. All sorts of horrible scenarios played across the screen in his mind. Was she hurt? Had Greg's killer returned after all? Ben should have listened to his instincts.

With fear coiling low in his belly, he sent out a text alert to the Rangers at lightning speed, then quickly changed from his drawstring sleep shorts into jeans and a T-shirt. Grabbing socks, tennis shoes and his sidearm, he ran from the apartment with his keys dangling from his fist.

He drove barefoot, taking the curves and running the traffic lights across town to the Pike ranch, the whole while mentally thrashing himself for having acquiesced to Corinna's insistence she stay at her house.

Guilt, ugly and feral, reared up to poke at his conscience. His actions may have put Corinna in harm's way. He'd never forgive himself if she were hurt again.

He pulled his Jeep to a halt next to Corinna's compact car and jumped out. Sharp bits of gravel dug into his bare feet but he ignored the pain. Lights lit up the house. He rushed to the front door and banged his fist against the wood. "Corinna!"

From his right, Corinna came tearing around the corner of the house, her dark hair flying loose around her shoulders, like a midnight cloud. She came to a skidding halt, her bare feet sliding slightly on the slick, dew-damp grass. Her eyes were wild and her body trembled violently beneath the plush softness of her pale blue robe.

She wasn't dead. Relief nearly brought him to

his knees. He vaulted off the porch and ran to her, drawing her close. She felt so brittle in his arms. His chest tightened with emotions he didn't want to take the time to examine.

"What happened?" he asked. He eased her back to look at her. "Are you hurt?"

She shook her head, her long brunette hair cascading over her shoulders in waves. "No. I'm fine. A man broke in and searched my father's office. What could he be looking for?"

His stomach dropped. She was still in danger. "I don't know. Did you see him?"

She stepped out of his embrace. "I caught a glimpse of him as he ran out the patio doors. I shot at him but missed. The bullet zoomed past and hit the wall. I chased after him but…" She shrugged with self-deprecation. "He wasn't encumbered with fuzzy slippers. Even barefoot, I couldn't catch him. He climbed the pasture fence and took off. I was afraid to shoot at him again because of the horses."

Not sure he heard correctly, he asked, "You shot at him? Then chased after him. What did you shoot with?"

"My gun, of course." From the folds of her robe she produced a 3-inch barreled, .45 caliber Micro Compact pistol.

Ben raised his eyebrows. "You carry a weapon?" A moment of surrealism overtook him. Seeing her with the weapon was so incongruent with his idea of her. He quickly relieved her of the piece.

She sliced him a sardonic look. "Dad insisted I know my way around a handgun. He always said, 'Just in case.' Well, tonight was a 'just in case' kind of night."

Ben couldn't have agreed more. But he'd had no idea Greg had armed his daughter. And he hated that she'd had to use the weapon. "I assume you have a safe or lock box for this?"

"Of course. In my room. I'm just bummed I didn't get the guy." A pained expression tightened her features. "Or had it on me earlier!"

He shuddered at the thought of her confronting either assailant. And to chase after this one! What had she been thinking?

If this was the same culprit who'd killed her father, he could have easily shot at her again. Why hadn't he? And where was the SAPD officer who'd been standing guard?

Ben decided he'd puzzle the questions out later. For now he had to stay focused on Corinna. This was his fault. He'd allowed her to be put in danger. He'd let his captain down.

Heart thudding in time with the pounding at his temple, he said, "I'm so sorry. I shouldn't have let you stay here."

Hugging her robe around her middle, she said, "You didn't have much say in the matter."

His jaw tightened. He'd made the mistake once of letting her talk him into going against his better judgment. There wouldn't be a repeat. Not on his watch.

Where was the police officer he'd had guarding her? "Did you see the SAPD officer?"

Her eyebrows pulled together. "I didn't."

The sound of squealing tires and car doors slamming announced the arrival of other Rangers.

Anderson Michaels thundered onto the porch. His blond hair was mussed and his sharp eyes were filled with concern. "You two okay?"

Ben nodded over the top of Corinna's head. "She's unhurt. Someone broke in and trashed the study. He ran out through the back patio doors. Like last time. The SAPD officer is missing."

Pulling his weapon from the back of his sweatpants, Anderson said, "I'll find him." He hurried around the corner of the house.

Another car barreled into the driveway. Gisella stepped out of her vehicle and rushed forward. "What happened?" she asked.

He quickly explained the situation, then turned to Corinna. "You should go change. I want to take you to SAPD to look through mug shots. Maybe we've caught a break."

"Good idea," Corinna said as she stepped onto the porch.

"Gisella, go with her," Ben ordered.

Corinna paused and threw an incredulous look over her shoulder at him. "I can manage changing my clothes on my own."

Of course she could, but he hated the thought of her alone and unprotected. He refrained from insisting, telling himself she'd be fine. They were all within earshot of her. "Sorry. Of course."

She stared at him for a moment with questions in her eyes before she fled inside.

He watched her go, anxious at having her out of his sight even for a brief moment.

Anderson returned, helping a semi-conscious officer along with him. He propped the still groggy man up on the porch. "Found him knocked out under a bush in the back."

Gisella flipped open her phone. "I'll call for a bus."

"What could the perp be looking for?" Ben asked. "We searched the place after Greg was killed and didn't find anything useful."

Anderson ran a hand through his hair. "Beats me. But the guy trashed the study. I wonder if he got what he came for before Corinna chased him away?"

"I suggest we search through everything again," Gisella said. "Though I have no idea what we're looking for."

"That's the million dollar question," Anderson replied.

Ben agreed. "You two take care of it. When the others arrive, explain what's happening. I'll take Corinna into the station."

"She's welcome to come to my place when you're done," Gisella said.

Relieved by the offer, Ben said, "I'll go tell her to pack her bags."

He entered the house and strode down the hall. Stopping in front of her closed door, he knocked.

"Yes?" Corinna replied.

"It's me."

The door opened. Corinna had changed into black leggings, a long tunic-style red blouse and flat sandals that emphasized the delicate structure of her feet. She'd braided her hair off to one side. Her pale complexion set off her wide, dark eyes. She was so petite and fragile-looking that Ben wanted to wrap her once again in his arms and shield her from the world.

Whoa! That was not what Greg had entrusted her to him for.

Ben didn't generally react in such a touchy-feely manner. Not even the few girlfriends he'd had over the years had elicited such a knee-jerk need in him to protect them the way Corinna did. But there was something about Corinna which evoked the response. Something he didn't understand.

He'd better get a handle on his attraction, his weakness for her. She was off-limits. Greg had made that clear. Ben would never dishonor Greg.

He stayed in the doorway. "You'll need to pack your bags. You can stay with Gisella until we catch this guy," he said, more brusquely than he'd intended.

She arched a winged eyebrow. "You're really going to tell me what to do?"

Didn't she understand her life was in danger? "Your safety is paramount."

Her eyes flashed. "No. Finding my father's killer is the priority."

He allowed a wry smile to tip the corner of his mouth. "Both are a priority. Solving your father's murder could take months unless we catch a break. Right now you are our best lead, which makes you a target. So the most pressing issue at this precise second is getting you somewhere safe."

Corinna considered his words, and then conceded his point with a slight incline of her head and a droop to her shoulders. "Fine. I'll pack a bag."

When he didn't make a move to leave the room, she came to stand in front of him. "I'm safe now. You and the others are here. There's no need for you to be so worried."

He captured her hands and held them. "I can't help it. If anything happens to you, I will never forgive myself."

Though she was sure she knew the answer, she asked anyway, "Why do you care so much?"

Two little creases formed between his eyebrows. "Because you're Greg's daughter. He's gone. It's up to me to protect you."

Unreasonable disappointment rushed over her. "Why you, specifically? Why not pass me off to one of the others?"

For a second, confusion darkened his hazel eyes. "I have to pass you off, as you say, to Gisella. For propriety's sake."

Hearing him confirm he was taking her

protection personally gave her an unexpected thrill. She shouldn't want his attention but she did. And knowing that he wanted not only to keep her safe, but to guard her reputation made tenderness tingle in her heart. "That's very old-fashioned of you. I'm sure my father would be proud."

Sadness crept into his expression. "Your father taught me a lot about values. And about faith. He was a great man."

She couldn't argue with that. She just wished her father had wanted to spend more time with her. Instead, he'd spent time with Ben. The old hurt throbbed. She withdrew her hands. "That still doesn't explain why you feel as though you have to be responsible for my safety. I'm sure any of the others would do just as well."

The corners of his mouth tightened slightly. "Greg asked me to look after you if anything should happen to him."

"Ah." Understanding smacked her upside the head. So she was his obligation. How idiotic of her to have harbored any thought he was taking such a personal interest for other reasons.

She was glad he'd put up the barrier between them. She'd let him protect her, while she protected her heart.

Quickly, she gathered her necessary belongings

into a couple of tote bags, the only thing she'd need to get was a toothbrush since she left hers out in the barn, and followed Ben out of the house to his Jeep.

"Oh, wait!" she said when she saw Gabby on the porch. Scooping up the feline, she turned to Gisella. "Is it okay if Gabby comes to your house as well?"

Gisella grimaced. "I'm sorry. I'm allergic to cats."

"Then my staying with you won't work." Corinna bit her lip. She could stay at the Miriam shelter she volunteered at, but as soon as the thought formed she rejected it. She wouldn't take a bed away from someone in need. "I could ask Susan or Felicia if I could stay with them."

"I don't think putting your friends in danger is a good idea," Ben said.

He was right, of course. She had no family left, no one to turn to. She was alone. The need to move, to dance, washed through her like a rogue wave. Only when she was dancing did she feel whole and in control. Agitation revved through her veins, her foot began to bounce. "I can stay at the dance studio. There's a couch in the locker room and I'm sure Madame wouldn't mind if Gabby's there."

Ben frowned. "No. Absolutely not."

"Then a pet-friendly hotel will have to do."

"I'd rather you stayed with Gisella. I'll take the cat."

Surprised, Corinna stared at him. "Really?"

"Yes. I'll take care of…"

"Gabby."

"Right. Gabby. I can have pets in my apartment."

She didn't even know where he lived, let alone why he'd offer, but she'd take it. "Thank you. Her food, dish and litter box are in the laundry room."

Relief softened Ben's jaw. "That's settled then. After we go to the station house, I'll take you to Gisella's."

Corinna glanced at the female Ranger. "You're kind to offer. Are you sure I wouldn't be putting you out?"

Gisella smiled. "Not at all. I'm between roommates at the moment. The second bedroom is furnished and unoccupied."

"It's a good plan," Ben said, taking one of Corinna's hands and squeezing. "Stay with Gisella. You'll be safe there."

Safe.

His hazel eyes implored her to accept the offer.

Part of her wanted to rebel, wanted to say no, she was strong enough, brave enough to stay here regardless of the danger. She didn't need their help. But she really wasn't foolish, either. She nodded.

After gathering her cat's belongings and stowing them away in the back of the Jeep, Ben drove them to the San Antonio Police station.

This early in the morning, with the first streaks of sunrise appearing on the horizon, the green glass and yellow-sided police department building was lit up from within. Crime didn't sleep and neither did the night shift officers.

After identifying himself, Ben explained the situation to the navy-and-gold-uniformed desk sergeant. They were led to a vacant desk in the belly of the bustling department.

"Have a seat," the sergeant said. "I'll bring you the books for the past five years."

"Perfect," Ben said as he held out a chair for Corinna.

She took a seat on the padded task chair while Ben grabbed a nearby metal folding chair, turned it around, and straddled the seat, looking directly at her. His gaze searched her face. The way he studied her was a bit unnerving. He'd been staring ever since they'd left her home.

If her dad hadn't been killed, she'd have been amused by Ben's overbearing way of ordering her to Gisella's. She usually didn't take to such high-handed behavior. But her father had been murdered and the recent break-in freaked her out.

The shot she'd fired off still had her ears ringing, and truth be told she was scared and feeling vulnerable. The intruder could have returned to kill her instead of searching for something. Ben had said the Rangers didn't know what the guy had been seeking. Neither did she.

"Here we go," the sergeant said, depositing a stack of five photo albums on the metal desktop in front of Corinna.

Each album was three inches thick. She flipped open the cover of the top one. The page was filled with small, square photos. There were hundreds of pictures to go through. It would be like looking for a viper in a pit full of every kind of snake imaginable. Her face must have betrayed her dismay at the enormity of the task facing her.

"I know this seems daunting, but take your time. Scan the photos. If anyone looks remotely familiar let me know," Ben said.

She nodded and settled herself to the task. An hour and five books later, she finally shook her head. "I don't know, Ben. He could be any number of these guys."

Disappointment seeped into her tone, but she couldn't help it. She'd so wanted to find the person responsible for her father's death. She wished she could simply point a finger to a photo and, presto, have their killer.

Ben put his hand on her arm. "Don't beat yourself up about this. You're tired. Maybe we can have you work with a sketch artist. Paige is great at coaxing details from people's subconscious. I'll have her drive over from Austin."

"I'll try anything," Corinna said, willing to do whatever it took to find her father's killer.

Ben rose. "Tomorrow after you've had some rest." He held out his hand. "Let's get you to Gisella's."

She slipped her hand into his engulfing grip and allowed him to help her to her feet. His fingers locked firmly around hers. Their palms meshed together, sending waves of sensation up her arm to settle in the vicinity of her heart. There was no denying her attraction to Ben.

Old hurt and anger tightened her breathing. She still remembered the day he'd walked into her life thirteen years ago. He'd been a lanky, somewhat surly nineteen-year-old who'd embodied all her teenage dreams. Until she'd realized he wasn't leaving. Then she'd come to resent him for invading her family. For taking her father's attention away. For being the son she couldn't be.

She jerked her hand free, ignoring his confused expression as she preceded him out of the police station into the still-dark and temperate morning air.

Attraction couldn't counteract all the years of resentment piled up in her heart like old moldy blankets, smothering in its intensity and weighing down any wayward, unwanted yearnings.

In the grand scheme of her life, giving in to her attraction to Ben would only bring her more pain.

She had to remember that.

FOUR

Corinna arrived at the San Antonio Dance Company's building and parked near the door. Thankfully, this early in the day no one was about. She'd quietly left Gisella's house before the Ranger had awoken.

Keeping an alert eye for any possible danger and her cell phone ready, she'd walked several blocks before calling a taxi to take her to her house so she could get her car. The thought of being cooped up, basically like a prisoner, in the Ranger's house had provoked the streak of rebellion that Corinna worked hard to keep at bay.

Her father always lamented her rebellious nature would one day get her in trouble. Ha! She'd lived her whole life doing what others wanted her to do. And she wasn't stupid. Her father had made sure she knew how to handle herself.

Since she tended to rehearse at odd hours when

others weren't in the building, she had a key to the side door. In the stillness of the early morning, she entered. The place was muggy from being locked up tight. She decided not to open any windows. Inside the studio room, she fired up the stereo system and did a quick warm-up before pushing play. Tchaikovsky's pas de deux sprang from the speakers to surround her. The notes so familiar, so cherished.

But her scattered thoughts wouldn't let her relish the music. Her father was dead. Gone forever.

A sob lay trapped in her throat.

Ben's words slammed into her mind. *You can count on all of the Rangers. We are your family now.*

She didn't want that. She'd lived too long in that world to stay there willingly. But where did she belong?

Here. She belonged here in this studio, doing the only thing she knew how to do.

Shutting down her mind and ignoring the bite of pain in her biceps, she allowed her body to flow to the music. Dancing had become her refuge during her youth. Today it was so much more. Losing herself to the movement, the music, insulated her from the outside world. Inside the bubble of dance, she was safe. There was no sorrow, there was no pain. Only the dance.

She caught a glimpse of her reflection in the mirrored wall. Who was that wild-eyed, pale ghost of a woman?

Tears blurred her vision. She squeezed her eyes tight. And pirouetted her way to oblivion.

A little before eight in the morning, Ben arrived at the Rangers' offices with a heavy heart. The flat-roofed, sprawling building looked unusually drab this morning, as if reflecting the grief tightening Ben's chest. He pulled into his usual spot next to Gisella's truck. All of the Rangers' vehicles were in their spots. All but one. Greg's wasn't there and never would be again.

As soon as Ben got out of his Jeep, a reporter descended.

"Can you confirm the identity of the fallen Ranger as Captain Gregory Pike?" the red-haired female reporter asked as she shoved a microphone into Ben's face.

Her eager-to-get-the-story expression drove a stake through Ben's heart. His blood pressure skyrocketed. The media had no soul, no understanding of human compassion, only a hunger to get the story no matter what the cost.

"No comment." He pushed past the cameraman angling to capture him on film.

Thankful to leave the reporter and her sidekick outside, Ben swiped his access card and entered the relatively quiet building. He took a moment to compose himself before making his way to his office. After checking his messages, he went in search of Marissa Franklin, the administrative assistant. He found her sitting at her desk staring out the window.

"Marissa," he said as he entered her workspace.

She wiped at her eyes before turning toward him. As always, she was dressed impeccably in a starched blouse and skirt. Her short, bobbed hair matched the warm brown color of her eyes. "How can I help you?"

Ben appreciated her professionalism though he knew she had to be hurting just as badly as the rest of them. Marissa had worked closely with Greg for the past few years. Respecting her need to keep emotions in check, he said, "I need the key to Greg's office."

Without blinking an eye at the request, she opened a drawer and withdrew a key ring. "Here you go. Senior Captain Parker is waiting in the conference room for you."

Not surprised to learn the senior captain was already here, Ben wished he had something concrete to report.

"Thank you." He turned to go, then paused. "Marissa, do you have any idea what case came up recently that Greg was working on?"

She shook her head. "I don't. But I can check the logs to see if anything came in that I'm unaware of."

"That would be helpful." Instead of heading directly to the conference room, Ben returned to his office where he called the Texas Department of Public Safety Crime Laboratory Service operating out of San Antonio.

"Talk to me, James," Ben said to the head technician when he got him on the phone.

"Hey, Ben. Sorry about Greg. He'll be missed."

A swell of sorrow rushed in. Ben gripped the receiver tighter. "Yes. What do we know so far?"

"The coroner is just starting his exam. I won't have the bullet for a few hours. I can tell you that the prints taken off the unknown vic don't show up in IAFIS."

Ben's jaw tightened painfully. The Integrated Automated Fingerprint Identification System used primarily by law enforcement agencies across the country was the largest biometric database in the world. Most people's fingerprints and corresponding information such as address and criminal record were entered into the system whether they realized it or not. Seemed this guy had somehow managed to avoid being fingerprinted. "What about DNA?"

"We've sent samples to the FBI's CODIS—the Combined DNA Index System—and we're running them here in our lab. We won't have results for at least seven to ten days."

Time was not on their side. Every minute that went by meant the criminal who'd shot Greg was on the loose and possibly getting away.

"But unless we find something to compare the data to, it's useless," James stated.

Taking a deep breath to stem the tide of frustration, Ben asked, "Anything else?"

"I sent photos of the vic to our Austin office. They have the most up-to-date facial recognition software available and are hooked into the National Crime Information Center database. Plus, Paige Bryant knows that system better than anyone else I've ever met. If the guy's image is in the cyber world, Paige will find it."

"Let's hope," Ben said. He'd only met the

forensic artist a few times and had liked her calm demeanor. He reminded himself to have her drive down to work with Corinna.

"We found particulates on the unknown vic. Some grass and pollen fibers. We're working on identifying them. We also found traces of clay loam on the floor after both incidents, which is indigenous to the area around the Pikes' place."

"We're pretty sure the perp came in through the patio doors and left the same way both times."

"Makes sense. But anyone or anything could have tracked in the loam. We also found cat hairs on Greg."

"His daughter, Corinna, has a cat."

"Okay." He sighed. "That's all I have for now."

"Keep me updated." As soon as he hung up, Ben dialed Paige's number. He explained what he needed. She agreed to drive down straight away. With his calls done, Ben ran a hand over his close-cropped hair, the ends bristling against his palm. Best to face the inevitable. He headed toward the large conference room where the Rangers convened to discuss active investigations.

All the Rangers were seated at the huge oval table. A sea of white hats, grim expressions and suppressed emotions awaited him. They were all grieving their captain's demise and anxious to catch the villain. Trevor slipped in behind Ben and took a seat. Ben stood and braced his hands on the back of an empty leather chair.

At the head of the table stood Texas Ranger Senior Captain Doug Parker, dressed in tan slacks, a navy sport coat over a white button-down and a white hat. In his late sixties, Parker made an imposing figure at six-one with a bony frame that barely contained the energy emanating from him.

The lines in his craggy face were as harsh as his sharp green eyes as he assessed the nine men and one woman in front of him from beneath the brim of his hat. He smoothed a finger over his handlebar mustache. "It's a sad, sad day," he said.

Nods of agreement went around the room.

"But we carry on. The Rangers have always carried on," Parker said in a solemn tone. "There's work to be done. First I need to appoint a new captain to Company D."

The sound of the Rangers shifting in their seats filled Ben's ears. He kept his gaze trained on Parker, though he could feel the speculative glances shooting his way.

Ben cleared his throat. "We need to find our

captain's murderer before any decisions are made."

Parker's eyes narrowed. "Without a leader the team will falter."

"I agree," Trevor interjected, his voice vibrating with anticipation. He stood. "As the senior lieutenant, I'm more than willing to step into the captain's role."

Parker never shifted his gaze from Ben. "Duly noted, Donovan. However, Lieutenant Fritz will be promoted to Captain of Company D."

The senior's words hit Ben like a fist to the solar plexus. He and Greg had talked about the day when Ben would be promoted, but it was always in the context of when Greg retired.

"What? How can you do this?" sputtered Trevor.

Parker pinned Trevor with his glittering eyes. "If you have a problem with the situation, we can discuss it in private." Turning his sharp gaze back to Ben, he said, "So, Fritz, do you accept the position?"

Ben's heart pounded. He wanted the promotion, but not like this. Greg should be the one handing off the leadership baton. But Greg was gone and Ben needed to face that fact. His gut crunched.

He glanced around the table, appreciating the

encouraging looks of the Rangers of Company D. Slowly, he nodded, accepting the responsibility out of respect for his fallen captain.

Parker nodded with satisfaction. "Good." His expression turned grim. "Then I'll leave you to find Pike's murderer. Anything you need, Ben, don't hesitate to ask. You have all of the resources of the State of Texas at your disposal." Parker touched the brim of his hat and headed for the door.

Ben hurried to catch up with him in the hall. "Captain Parker, I'd like to request to promote Daniel Riley to the rank of lieutenant."

Parker stopped and placed a hand on Ben's shoulder. "I think that's a fine idea. Fill out the necessary forms."

"Thank you, sir."

Sadness crept into the older man's eyes. "I'm sorry about Greg. I know you two were close."

"We were, sir." As close as father and son. Only their bond went deeper. Ben had trusted Greg with his life. And vice versa. If only Ben had arrived twenty minutes earlier….

Parker squeezed Ben's shoulder. "I have every confidence you'll bring the murderer to justice. And until the fiend is apprehended, you are charged with keeping Corinna Pike safe."

"I will," Ben assured him with rock solid determination strengthening his tone. "Believe me, I will."

Trevor stepped out into the hall. "Captain Parker, may I have a word?"

Parker removed his hand from Ben's shoulder, sighed and then nodded to the other Ranger. "Walk with me, Donovan."

Shooting Ben a withering glare, Trevor edged past him and walked away with Captain Parker.

Ben reentered the conference room and accepted his comrades' well wishes with bittersweet emotion. He held up a hand and waited until they quieted down. "Where are we in the investigation? I want this guy caught before he comes after Corinna since she can ID him."

"Still waiting on forensics to identify more trace elements found at the scene after the break-in," Oliver said.

"We should have the ME's report by noon," Gisella said.

"The neighbors didn't see or hear a thing," Levi said. "We found several sets of tire tracks at the back gate. Hard to say if they were fresh or not. Took impressions and gave them to forensics. Still waiting."

"Hurry them along." Ben turned his gaze to

Daniel and Marvel. "And the man found shot with Greg?"

"Coma guy? No change," Marvel replied. "SAPD sent over two officers. They'll report in if there's any development."

Disappointment lodged a boulder in his chest. "So basically, we have squat."

An uncomfortable silence fell across the room.

"Come on, people. No one can be that good. Our killer had to mess up somehow. We just have to find his mistake." Ben prayed his words were true. Turning to Anderson, he asked, "What does the SAPD officer from last night have to say?"

"Not much. Guy came up from behind him and hit him over the head with a rock from the garden," Anderson replied.

"Prints?"

Anderson shook his head. "Guy wore gloves."

"Figures," Ben said. He shifted his gaze to another Ranger seated at the table. "Oliver, when Paige arrives, see if the facial recognition software has come up with an ID for coma guy."

"Will do, Captain." Oliver grinned. "I sure like the sound of that."

Ben wished he could fully embrace his new title,

but his grief was too fresh. He'd give anything to have Greg back. "Thanks."

His gaze swept over the remaining Rangers. "Beat the bushes. Find something useful. Cade, check with the DA. See if any of Greg's old cases send up any red flags. We have to work this from every angle. The guy's still out there and Corinna could be his next target."

"On it, boss," Cade said as he slipped his cell phone out of his sport-coat pocket. He rose and left the conference room.

Ben headed for Greg's office. He unlocked the door and flipped on the overhead light. A long filing cabinet ran the length of the room beneath the large rectangular window overlooking the back parking lot. The mahogany desk facing the door was neat, just the way Greg liked it, with files piled on the corner edge, pens in their holder and a computer waiting to be booted up.

Behind the desk, the rust-colored, high-back leather chair beckoned for its owner to sit. Ben wasn't that man.

How could he ever measure up to his mentor and friend's legacy? Greg had been a fierce leader, determined to right wrongs and bring order out of chaos. He'd taught Ben how to exert power without aggression, how to remain calm in the face of deadly situations and how to uphold the law while upholding justice because the two didn't always coincide.

Greg's certificates covered the wall facing Ben. College diplomas, academy documents, Ranger credentials. Pieces of a man's life.

Shaking off the melancholy threatening to cut off his breath, Ben moved behind the desk. With a slight hesitation, he sat in the leather chair. As difficult as this situation was, he had an investigation to conduct. He was Captain now.

Get on with it, he admonished himself.

With determination, he booted up the computer. It didn't take long to figure out the password—Corinna. Ben opened the top drawer and examined the contents—pens, paperclips, stacks of sticky notepads, official forms.

Which reminded Ben that he wanted to get Daniel's promotion in the works right away.

He found what he needed in the stack he pulled from the drawer and filled in the blanks. The desk phone rang just as he finished.

For a long moment he stared at the instrument as if he'd never seen a phone before. Finally, he picked up the receiver. "Fritz."

The administrative assistant's voice came over the line. "You have a call on line one."

"Thanks, Marissa." He depressed the blinking light. "Captain Fritz."

"This is SAPD Officer Talbot. Sir, we have a situation here at the hospital."

FIVE

Adrenaline spiked through Ben. "He woke up?"

"No, sir. We have a Corinna Pike here demanding to talk to the unconscious man. She said you'd know her."

Surprise rushed in, pushing the adrenaline to the background. "I do. I'm on my way."

What was she doing there? And asking to talk to the victim? How crazy was that? She had no business involving herself in his investigation.

The question rattled inside his head as he hung up and glanced at Gisella, who stood in the doorway of Greg's office. "Corinna's at the hospital wanting to see coma guy," Ben said.

Surprise flickered in her dark eyes. "I assumed she was still asleep in her room when I left this morning. I should have looked in on her. There's an SAPD officer stationed outside my house.

They'd have informed me if she'd left. How did she get to the hospital?"

Frustration pounded at his temple. "I have no idea."

"I can go," Gisella offered.

Rising from the chair, Ben shook his head. "No. I'll take care of her. She's my responsibility."

Gisella arched an eyebrow.

For some reason, heat crept up Ben's neck. "Was there something you needed?"

"I was just going to give you a quick update on her," she replied.

"How did she seem to you?"

"She's taking her father's death hard, as one would expect. She wasn't happy when I told her she needed to stay inside the house at all times."

Picturing her bleak eyes when they'd parted last, he didn't know how she'd survive after such a loss. And now she'd left the safety of Gisella's home, putting herself in needless danger when the assassin was still at large and probably knew she could ID him. The need to see her, to protect her, spurred him on.

"Call my cell if you need me," he said before hurrying from the office.

He encountered little traffic on his way to the

hospital. Rather than wait for the elevator, he took the stairs and emerged on the fourth floor opposite the nurses' station. He tipped his hat in greeting and hastened down the hall. The smell of antiseptic burned his nose. The soft noises of the hospital echoed inside his head as he neared Corinna.

She looked fragile and beautiful and in need of protection. Her leather-soled shoe tapped soundlessly against the linoleum, and her slender arms were wrapped around her middle. She wore jeans and a plum-colored tank top. Her dark, silky hair was captured at her nape in a twist, emphasizing her slender neck and porcelain skin. Her eyes were wide and filled with desperation in the swirling depths.

The stark white bandage taped to her bare biceps reminded him of how close she had come to being killed. His heart contracted painfully.

Acknowledging the two haggard-looking SAPD officers with a tip of his head, he led her away by the elbow. "Corinna, what are you doing here? You were supposed to stay at Gisella's."

"I couldn't just sit there doing nothing," she said, her voice breaking.

He could see how badly she was hurting. He wished he could make her feel better. But he didn't know how to accomplish such a feat. "How did you get here?"

She tugged on her bottom lip with her teeth before answering. "I called a taxi and went home to get my car."

"But how did you get past the SAPD officer?"

"He probably hadn't arrived yet. I left Gisella's around six this morning."

A fist of aggravation and anxiety slammed into his midsection. He was going to have to do a better job of protecting her, not only from her father's killer but from herself. He sought an even tone as he said, "We can't protect you if you're sneaking off and running around alone."

A little crease appeared between her eyebrows. "I don't need to ask permission to live my life."

"But we can't protect you if we don't know what you're doing."

Through gritted teeth, she said, "I can take care of myself."

And the state's Ten Most Wanted would meet him for coffee tomorrow morning. She was lean, bordering on too thin, petite with delicate features. A strong wind could blow her over.

He pushed back his hat and rubbed at his pounding temple. "Corinna—"

She cut him off in a voice that shook with suppressed emotion. "Tell them to let me in there." Her sorrowful brown eyes implored him to understand. "I want him to tell me who shot my father."

"He hasn't come out of his coma," he stated gently.

Her pretty lips pressed together in a straight line. She took a breath and slowly let it out. "I understand that. But I read online that sometimes coma victims can still hear and rouse to respond to what's being said to them. Maybe…" She took another shuddering breath. "Maybe he'll want to wake up to tell us who shot him. And my father."

Ben had thought the same thing. He'd tried, but nothing happened.

An inner nudging made him pause. If the man in the bed could hear, maybe listening to the woman who'd tried to save him, the daughter of the other victim, might be the catalyst to bring him back to consciousness. Who was Ben to deny her the attempt?

"Let me check with the doctor. If he says yes, then I'll take you in there," he said.

Her face lit up with hope.

His stomach dropped. "You can't get your hopes up. This is a long shot and may not work."

"But it could."

Her desperate expression beseeched him to believe along with her. He wanted to. He wanted the man to wake up. But he was realistic enough to know not everything turned out the way one wanted or hoped.

After securing the doctor's permission, Ben sent up a silent prayer he wasn't making a mistake by allowing Corinna to go into the room.

She'd suffered too many traumas already. He wasn't sure she could sustain any more.

Corinna walked into the hospital room, acutely aware of Ben's hand on the small of her back, the warmth reassuring. She glanced over her shoulder at him. He towered over her five-foot-four frame. Compassion and determination etched lines in his attractive face. He was handsome, she'd give him that. Dressed in pressed cotton slacks, a pale green dress shirt and sporting a fancy tie, he radiated strength.

Just as her father had. And look what good all his strength had gotten him. Dead.

With a shudder she marched forward. They had five minutes, the doctor had grudgingly stated. She had a feeling that Ben's powers of persuasion had something to do with the doctor's acquiescence.

In the bed, hooked up to tubes and monitors, lay the man she'd found wounded in her father's study. He looked much different now—cleaned-up, pale and at the mercy of the doctors. Empathy formed a tight knot deep inside of her. "Do you know who he is?"

"No. We've been unable to ID him so far. I'm still waiting for the facial recognition software database to come up with a name."

She moved to the side of the bed. Careful of the IV attached to the back of his hand, she closed her fingers over the man's and leaned close. "My name is Corinna Pike. I'm the woman who found you last night."

Anticipation gripped her chest. "You were in my house with my father, Ranger Greg Pike. Someone shot you. Can you please wake up and tell us who did this to you? Who shot you? Who shot my father? I need to know who killed my father." She waited, peering at him for some sign that he'd heard her.

Nothing. His face remained unresponsive.

Ben shifted closer and placed a hand on her shoulder. She shrugged him off. Desperation clawed at her. Her throat burned and tears rolled down her cheeks and dropped on to the blanket covering the injured man. "Please. I beg of you. Wake up!"

Still nothing. Disappointment gathered steam. She put her other hand on his shoulder and gave a sharp shake. "Wake up."

"Corinna," Ben said in a gentle reprimand.

She released the unresponsive John Doe and stepped back, her clenched fists tight at her sides.

"We need to give him time to heal," he said.

"But what if he never regains consciousness? He's the only one who knows what happened."

She turned to face Ben. There was little doubt that whoever had killed her father had done so because he was a Texas Ranger. They were men and women who faced danger daily, while their loved ones waited in the wings and worried. Then grieved.

She would never live that life again. Not when she knew God wouldn't answer her prayers for protection. As long as she'd thought God was watching over her father, she had refused to let the deadly reality of his job paralyze her.

Now…fear wanted to devour and destroy.

But it had an accomplice: the unknown.

Ben touched her arm. "I'm going to catch your father's murderer with or without this man's help. And I'm not going to let you get hurt, either."

Resolve to do all she could to help catch her father's killer sprouted roots in her soul and spread shoots of anger through her, spearing her fears.

Somehow, someway, they'd find the person responsible.

Ben led her away from the unconscious man. "Come on, let's go where we can sit and talk." Outside the room, Ben said to the officers standing guard, "Thank you, gentlemen. Let me know immediately if there's any change."

Corinna allowed Ben to guide her through the hospital corridors. Ben pushed open a door and led her through a dimly lit room to a larger area. The high ceiling, wooden bench pews and sunlight filtering in through intricately carved stained glass windows brought Corinna to awareness. Ben had brought her to the hospital chapel.

Everything inside her rebelled.

She halted on the threshold to the sanctuary. "No. No, I can't be here."

He captured her hand. "Sit with me. Pray with me."

Shaking her head, she backed away, but he held her tethered to him. "I can't."

"Corinna, let God comfort you."

"No!" She yanked her hand free and moved back into the vestibule. "I don't want anything to do with God. Not now. I prayed every day of my life for Him to protect my father, but He allowed this to happen." She wiped furiously at the tears streaming down her face. "Why? Why did He allow this to happen?"

Pain flickered in Ben's deep brown eyes. "Corinna, God didn't do this. A human did. A man..." He paused as if a thought had just occurred to him. "Or a woman killed your father and shot that guy laying in a coma. And lest you forget, whoever it was took a crack at you, too."

"I know God didn't physically kill my father, but He could have protected him. My father believed, he had a deep faith. Why didn't God save him?"

"Your father *was* saved. You have to believe he's in heaven now."

"I don't know what I believe anymore," she said, frustrated that he didn't understand the sense of betrayal burning inside of her. "I don't understand why God didn't protect Dad here on Earth."

Ben sighed, his expression full of sorrow. "I don't have an answer for you. But I do know that God is good and there is evil in this world." His expression implored her to understand. "Evil did this, not God."

A deep aching pain pressed on her lungs until she thought she'd choke. She had to get out of the chapel, away from Ben and his well-meaning words that didn't answer her questions about God or offer any relief from the pain of being set adrift from all the certainties in her life. "I've got to go. I can't…."

Ben's expression stilled, frozen in mute wretchedness. He reached out to stop her, but she hurried from the chapel and through the hospital until she was outside in the late morning sun. She knew Ben wasn't far behind.

She gasped for breath. She couldn't seem to draw in air. Ben's words echoed inside her head. *Evil did this, not God.*

But God could have stopped it, her mind screamed.

Not waiting for Ben to catch up, she ran for her car and drove to the dance studio, the only place where she could retreat, where she could be free of the tormenting question. But somehow she doubted she'd ever be able to erase the look of heartbreak she'd seen on Ben's face when she'd turned away from his offer of comfort.

And it tore at her heart.

Ben followed closely behind Corinna's car all the way to the studio to make sure she arrived safely. He didn't understand her reluctance to allow God to offer her comfort. It made no sense. Ben knew that Greg and Corinna were committed to their faith. Greg had shown Ben the true meaning and power of believing in God. To know Corinna was questioning her faith hurt Ben deeply. One more way Ben would be letting Greg down if Corinna lost her faith.

He pulled his Jeep into a spot a few spaces down from Corinna's car. He debated going into the dance studio after her. Would she rebuff or welcome his effort?

Deciding his promise to watch over her took precedence over their feelings, he went inside the small crowded lobby. A variety of dancers milled around. Some stretching. Others quietly talking.

Corinna stopped short, frowned and hurried to his side. "What now?"

"You should return to Gisella's," he stated, keeping his voice low so only she'd hear him.

"We don't know if you're out of danger. That guy could come after you again."

She glanced around and then waved him away from the congregating dancers. "I'm safe here. Look around you. No one is going to try something with so many witnesses."

He looked around. She *would* be surrounded by people. But that didn't mean she was safe. "How long?"

"I don't know. A couple of hours and then I'm headed to Miriam's for the rest of the day."

"Miriam's?"

"It's a shelter for battered women and children. We're having a benefit recital to raise money so the shelter can remodel their kitchen and purchase more beds."

Ah. That Miriam's. He hadn't known she was involved so closely with a charity. Especially a faith-based ministry like Miriam's. "What do you do there?"

"Most of my volunteer time is spent giving dance lessons to the children."

Impressed, he said, "How long have you been helping out there?"

"Since before college."

A long time. "Very admirable, Miss Pike."

Her cheeks pinkened. "Thanks. Look, I've got to go rehearse. You're not going to stay here, are you?"

"What time are you going to the shelter?"

"I'm usually there from noon until four." Her eyebrows scrunched together. "Though I would like to visit Gabby today."

"Are you sure you're up for rehearsing? Considering." He gestured toward her biceps where the white square bandage covered the evidence of the violence she'd suffered.

Her gaze slid to her arm. She closed her eyes for a moment. When she opened them, determination lit up the dark depths. "My father would be the first person to say I shouldn't wallow. I can't just do nothing. I'll go crazy."

He understood. He was itching to get out there and track down a murderer. "I'll have SAPD send a cruiser to patrol the area and I'll meet you at your car at noon."

For a moment he thought she was going to argue with him, but then she sighed. "I'll see you then."

With a tip of his hat, he watched her hurry into one of the dance studios. Once outside, he pulled out his phone and made the necessary arrangements with the San Antonio Police Department, then returned to Ranger headquarters. He put

Corinna at the back of his mind so he could concentrate on finding the person responsible for destroying the Pike family. Or at least he tried.

Corinna's arm ached something fierce by the time she was finished rehearsing. After two strenuous sessions she wasn't surprised. Because of the painful wound and the sorrow consuming her heart, she didn't think she could manage not to cry in front of the children at Miriam's.

She sent a silent plea for forgiveness upward, to her father, to God, she didn't know which. She wasn't strong enough not to wallow just a little more.

She arranged for another dancer to cover her classes at the shelter for the rest of the week. Though the shelter didn't pay, teaching the children was such a joy. Watching them learn to fouetté, plié and jeté across the floor melted her heart. It was hard to let go, to ask for help, but she had to do what was best for the kids.

As she left the dance studio and all the offers of condolences behind, she also acknowledged Ben had been right. She should have stayed at Gisella's for a few days before venturing out. Accepting the sympathy of others while trying to maintain her composure was exhausting.

Ben was waiting as promised by her compact car. Concern darkened his expression. "You look wiped out."

It grated to agree with him. "Yeah, I am. I won't be going back to the shelter this week."

Approval lit his eyes. "That's wise."

His appreciation twisted her up inside. She wasn't sure if she liked it or resented it. She turned away to open her car door. "Can you take me to see Gabby now?"

"Of course. Follow me."

Keeping pace with Ben's Jeep wasn't hard. The man drove well under the speed limit. Was that for her benefit? Or was he always so cautious?

She followed him to an apartment complex. The well-kept grounds and pristine buildings were upscale. She wasn't sure what she'd expected. A few mothers with youngsters in strollers walked along a paved path rimming the property. Here and there were other signs of children, a Big Wheel on the porch of one apartment, a doll sitting on the steps of another. Clearly this was a family-oriented place. She peeked at Ben. Was he the settle-down type, not the swinging-bachelor type? Her palms began to sweat.

Ben led the way to his upstairs unit and he opened the door and motioned her inside.

Curiosity propelled her forward. What kind of home did he keep? Was he a neatnik? Or would his place be the stereotypical bachelor pad? Somehow, she doubted it.

She found his apartment tidy, yet lived in. The leather couch showed signs of age in the distressed patches. A well-loved armchair looked invitingly comfortable. The beige carpet beneath the shocking-red area rug showed signs of being freshly vacuumed. The opposite wall was dominated by a plasma screen.

"Gabby," she called out as the bookcase next to the television drew her attention. She made kissing noises that usually enticed the cat to see what was going on.

Ben's books were a mixture of contemporary fiction titles alongside worn-leather classics. But it was the framed photos on the shelves that captured her interest. A photo of her father and Ben on a fishing trip. Another of a hunting excursion. Photos of various Christmases and Thanksgivings at her house. She was in several photos alongside her father. Her family was his family. Her throat tightened. There would never be another photo opportunity with her father again.

Her gaze snagged on an item sitting prominently on the top shelf. A medium-sized globe made of wood and polished brass. A gift she'd given to Ben a few years ago. Her father had insisted they give a present to Ben as well as to each other every year. Usually she'd let her father buy Ben's gift since she had no idea what Ben would want or need and really had no interest in finding out.

But this particular year, her father had been tied up with work and had asked her to pick the gift. She'd seen the globe in a little boutique on the Riverwalk. For some reason, she'd felt compelled to buy it. She could still remember the smile on Ben's face when he opened the box. And could remember the way that smile had made her feel proud that she'd found something he liked. It had been at odds with her feelings for Ben. Did he know she'd chosen it just for him?

"Here she is," Ben said, drawing her attention. The tabby ambled over and wound around her legs.

Bending down, she scooped up the cat. "Hi, baby."

The cat purred in response.

"Can I get you anything to drink?" Ben asked heading toward the kitchen.

"I don't want to keep you from…" the words *finding my father's killer* stuck in her throat. "Your job."

She put Gabby down and followed him. Even Ben's kitchen was orderly. No breakfast dishes in the sink, no crumbs on the counter. The chrome appliances shone as if recently wiped down.

"You're not." He grabbed a bottle of water from the refrigerator and held it up.

Taking the bottle, she noticed another framed photo on the kitchen wall. This one was from her college graduation party. She and Ben flanked her father. Corinna had been upset when her father insisted Ben be in the photo. This was her big day, she hadn't wanted to share it with Ben. But now looking at the picture, she'd give anything to go back to her grad night. She'd endure anyone and anything to have her father back.

"We should talk about your father's funeral."

His words slammed into her stomach as solidly as a fist. She didn't want to think about a funeral. Didn't want to think about saying goodbye. But she knew it had to be done.

She nodded and numbly walked into the living room. She sat on the couch. He took a seat in the armchair. "Did your father have a will?"

"He did. I'm sure our family lawyer, Marsden Boyle, will have a copy."

"Do you know what your father's wishes were for his burial?"

She swallowed the bile rising to burn her throat. "No. That wasn't something we talked about."

Ben nodded. "Most people don't. I believe your dad has a plot next to your mother."

"Yes, you're right." As did she. A shudder ran over her limbs. "I'm sure he'd want his pastor to do the service. Would you mind contacting him?"

"Not at all." Ben contemplated her a moment. "I can talk with the funeral home as well and take care of everything for you if you'd prefer."

She looked away to blink back tears. "I would, thank you."

Meow.

Gabby hopped onto the couch beside Corinna. Thankful for her cat, Corinna gathered her in her arms and buried her face in the soft fur.

"Corinna, if this is too painful, we can talk more about it later," Ben said.

Lifting her head, she said, "I just can't believe he's really gone."

Ben moved to sit beside her. He slid an arm around her and pulled her to his chest. "You'll get through this. We'll all get through this."

She wanted to believe Ben. But she feared her world was cracking into a million jagged pieces and if she weren't careful, she'd shatter too.

SIX

"Is he always so…" Corinna looked for the right word. She wasn't sure how to describe Ben. "Protective? Compulsively neat? Efficient?"

Gisella laughed. "You've known him longer than I have, don't you know?"

"Not really." Corinna reached for the popcorn bowl. They were sitting on the couch in Gisella's living room watching a chick flick, but Corinna's mind wasn't on the movie. She was thinking about Ben. About how solicitous he'd been from the beginning of this nightmare. About how protective and accommodating he was. She knew he was hurting just as badly as she was but he didn't show it.

She supposed the axiom that men compartmentalize their emotions had to be true. At least in Ben's case.

"What do you mean, not really?" Gisella asked, her dark eyes alight with curiosity.

Corinna picked at the popcorn, crumbling the fluffy kernels between her fingers and letting the crumbs fall to the napkin in her lap. "I've known him a long time but I don't really know him. What's he like at work?"

"Protective, compulsively neat, efficient," Gisella replied with a grin.

Corinna threw a piece of popcorn at her. "That's helpful."

Gisella sobered and paused the movie. "Really, Ben's a good guy. Your father thought highly of him. All the Rangers do."

Corinna knew just how highly her father had thought of Ben. He'd been the golden boy. The one whom her father preferred. Bitter anger churned in her gut. She tried to ignore it. Ben had been so solicitous and caring the past few days as they all coped with the loss of her father. "It must be hard on the company to be without a captain."

Gisella gave her a funny look. "Ben was promoted to captain. Didn't he tell you?"

"No." But why would he? They weren't friends. Not really. She wasn't sure what their relationship was. Or why he'd been so caring toward her. She knew she hadn't been the kindest and most thoughtful person when he was around. She wondered if he knew that she resented his intrusion into her and her father's life.

It didn't matter now. Her father was gone.

She set the popcorn aside. "Do you mind if I bail on you? I'm suddenly really tired."

"Not at all," Gisella said, her eyebrows drawing together. "Let me know if I can do anything for you."

"Thanks." Corinna rose and headed toward the spare room Gisella had loaned her. She hoped she'd find some sleep because she knew tomorrow she'd need her strength. Tomorrow she and Ben would be working together to put the final touches on the funeral arrangements. Not a task she was looking forward to.

A part of her longed to reach out to God for solace. To ask for help, strength, comfort. But she couldn't. Her heart felt hard within her chest. A cold stone where warmth once had surged.

Maybe turning to stone was what it was going to take to survive this.

A scratching noise brought Corinna out of a deep sleep. She lay immobile on the bed. Her mind mentally cataloged her surroundings. She was at Gisella's, in the spare bedroom. Dresser

to the left, door to the right. A window sat opposite from the bed. The blinds were drawn closed
and artificial light from the street lamp outside
shone through the side cracks. For a moment, she
wondered if she'd dreamt the noise.

A shadow passed by the crack, momentarily
blotting out the light seeping in. The scratching
resumed. Alarm jolted her heart rate. Someone
was trying to get in through the window. She
bolted from the bed and ran to Gisella's room.
She rapped on the door before bursting in.
"Gisella!"

The Ranger sat up and turned on the bedside
lamp. "Corinna? What's wrong?"

"I think someone's trying to get in through my
window."

Gisella threw back the covers, jumped from
the bed in her shorts and T-shirt and retrieved
her sidearm from the drawer of her nightstand.
"Stay here," she ordered as she hurried from the
room.

Corinna hated the helpless feeling stealing over
her as she sank to the floor and waited for the
Ranger to return. A prayer rose but she squashed
it. Why pray when she didn't think God would
listen?

Time ticked slowly by. The silence closed in on

Corinna. What was happening? Had the Ranger confronted the person trying to break in? Was she in trouble and in need of help?

Corinna rose on shaky legs and was about to open the bedroom door when Gisella came back, looking grim.

"Guy ran off. The SAPD officer gave chase but lost him." She put her weapon back into the drawer. "He'd removed the screen and was working to jimmie the window lock."

Corinna shuddered. "Maybe I should go somewhere else. I don't want to put you in danger."

Gisella gave her a funny look. "Uh, that's what I get paid the big bucks for. Don't worry. You're safe here. SAPD will double the security. Tomorrow I'll get bolt locks for all the windows."

"Why do you think he tried to break in here? What does he want with me?"

"You can ID him."

"Right." Which gave them the upper hand.

And hopefully that much closer to bringing the guy to justice.

But justice wouldn't bring her father back. Heavy sorrow weighted her down as she returned to her room and tried for sleep that never came. Especially after Gisella called Ben and insisted Corinna talk to him. He'd sounded frantic and she'd been adamant he not come over, saying she really needed to sleep. She hadn't wanted to deal with him fussing over her when there was nothing he could do anyway. Of course, he hadn't listened to her and she'd heard him arrive a short time later, but she feigned sleep. She wasn't sure when he finally left.

Later the next afternoon, Corinna steeled herself to see Ben as he pulled into the driveway of Gisella's house.

"Were you able to get some rest after this morning's scare?" Ben asked as Corinna slid into the passenger seat. He peered at her with concern.

She stuffed her gym bag with her dance clothes inside, beneath her feet. "So-so."

"This will be over soon. We'll catch the guy," he said softly.

She blinked back sudden tears, hating how close to the surface they were. She missed her father terribly. She despaired that no amount of time would heal the empty space in her life. The haunting image of her father's dead body tortured her mind. She focused her gaze on the afternoon traffic in an attempt to clear her thoughts.

At the Rangers' headquarters Ben escorted her to the conference room. She was acutely aware of his hand at the base of her back, the slight pressure both reassuring and chaotic to her system. She wanted to turn to him and curl into his embrace and forget that the world and its evil existed.

But she didn't.

She wanted to be tougher than that. She wanted to stand on her own two feet, not lean on a man, even one like Ben. She wanted to be her father's daughter. Strong and courageous. And in control.

When they stepped inside the conference room, she moved away from him. Better to not to have him touching her so she could think.

Corinna smiled at the lone woman sitting at the big oval table. She was pretty with wispy brunette hair and wide green eyes. Next to an open laptop computer on the table, a sketch pad and pencil waited.

Ben made the introductions.

Corinna offered the other woman her hand. "Nice to meet you, Paige. Thank you for coming down to San Antonio on such short notice."

"I didn't mind at all." She touched Corinna's hand and said, "I'm so sorry about your father."

Swallowing back a lump of sorrow, Corinna murmured, "Thank you."

Paige gathered her materials. "Shall we get to work?"

Ben held out a chair for Corinna. When she was seated, he said, "I'll be back in a bit. If you need anything, let me know. I'll be in my—your father's—office."

For a moment his expression crumbled, revealing the heartache he was trying so hard to hide.

Her own sorrow answered by thumping against her ribs and burning the backs of her eyelids. Against her will, Corinna's heart twisted with pain and empathy. Gisella had told her Ben had been promoted to captain. The news had hurt at first, more concrete evidence her father was gone, but it was selfish not to wish Ben well. And clearly he was uncomfortable assuming her father's office as his own.

She touched his arm before he could turn away. "It's your office now. I know Dad would be proud to have you taking over. It's what he groomed you for."

Ben laid a hand over hers and gave a slight squeeze. "Thank you."

She held his gaze until she couldn't stand to see her own anguish reflected in the hazel depths. Swallowing hard, she drew her hand back and studied her nails.

"Ladies," Ben said and exited the room.

Corinna focused on Paige and the task that needed to be accomplished. "So how do we do this?"

Paige explained and Corinna tried to recall the man she'd shot at the night before.

Paige paused with her pencil hovering above the paper. "Were his eyes wide set or closer together?"

"I don't—" Frustrated with her memory, Corinna shrugged. "I can't say for sure. I barely caught a glimpse of him."

Paige smiled, her brown eyes gentle. "I know this is difficult. Can you close your eyes and visualize the moment you saw him?"

With a sigh, Corinna closed her eyes and thought back to the split second when the man, outlined by the moon against the open patio doors, had turned to face her. "His eyes were not wide set. But not too close together either."

"Were they round or almond-shaped?"

"More almond-shaped but wide at the center. And dark. The man was definitely Hispanic." Corinna opened her eyes, excited to remember a few details. "He had a high forehead and his eyebrows were bushy."

Paige's hand moved quickly, the scratch of

pencil scraping against paper the only sound in the room. When Paige turned the sketch around, she said, "Something like this?"

Corinna studied the image of a man's face. Was he the man who'd broken into her home? She bit her lip in uncertainty.

The drawing showed an oval face, bushy eyebrows, a high forehead and oval eyes. Very generic features. Paige had penciled in straight, short hair swept back. The man seemed familiar but then again…she'd looked through hundreds of mug shots and so many had seemed familiar. "It could be. But I couldn't swear to it in a court of law."

"If Ben can catch this guy and he has the murder weapon that killed Captain Pike, then you won't have to testify," Paige said matter-of-factly.

But if the murder weapon wasn't found, linking the man who'd broken into her father's house to the murder, then Corinna's testimony could be the only thing standing in the way of his freedom. She couldn't make a mistake.

Doing so could cost her her life.

She wished she could pray for God to orchestrate the killer's downfall. But she'd given up hope that God listened to her prayers.

She'd just have to trust in Ben's ability to do his job. And hope Ben got to the killer before he got to Corinna.

Ben sat at the mahogany desk, in front of him were several stacks of files that needed to be reviewed—a few from Greg's office at the station and many from his home office. He'd cleared out the file cabinet and the desk drawers at both places, but so far hadn't found any clues that revealed what his captain had been working on. They'd searched Greg's office in the Pike house once again after this latest break-in, but still, nothing.

Every minute ticking by meant the killer was that much closer to getting away with murder.

Dropping his head into his hands, Ben prayed. "Please, Lord, let me find something, anything, which will lead us to the person who killed my friend and mentor. I ask this in Your Son's name, amen."

"Do you always pray when you're working?"

He lifted his head to find Corinna standing in the doorway. A piece of paper fluttered in her hand. Awareness of how angry she was at God made Ben want to tread tenderly.

He nodded. "I pray whenever I feel the need.

I know God listens no matter where I am. Your father taught me as much."

The derision in her expression left no doubt she disagreed and that pained him. She shrugged as she walked farther into the office. Her snug capri pants, loose-fitting blouse and sandals emphasized her diminutive stature. She appeared younger than her twenty-five years with dark circles under her eyes marring her porcelain-pale complexion.

He gestured to the paper she held. "May I see the sketch?"

She glided forward, her gaze taking in the desk and the wall full of her father's achievements. Her mouth tightened as if she were trying hard to keep her emotions held back.

Sympathy swelling, Ben rose and rounded the desk. Compelled by the need to touch her, he laid a hand on her bare arm, her skin warm, her bones so delicate. "Are you holding up?"

"Yes." The single word held a world of hurt and anguish.

His chest tightened. He wrapped his arms around her, offering her what comfort he could, knowing it wasn't nearly enough. How did he soothe away the loss of a parent? He couldn't. And he was a fool to try.

For a split second, she seemed to melt, but just

as quickly, she became rigid, withdrawing into herself before pulling out of his arms. He let his hands drop to his sides, unsure why her rejection hurt. It wasn't like he had any emotional investment in her other than his promise to Greg.

Yeah, sure, he thought she was beautiful in the way one thought a sparkling piece of jewelry behind a glass case was beautiful. And he certainly didn't want anything bad to happen to her.

But he didn't understand why every time she was around he felt compelled to draw her to him, to shield her, to make her hurt go away. He decided it was only because she seemed so vulnerable and fragile, as if any second she'd shatter into a million pieces. He couldn't let that happen.

"Here." She set the sheet of paper on the desk.

Shifting his focus back to business, he picked the paper up. The face staring up at him could have been any number of men walking around the streets of San Antonio, or all of Texas, for that matter. But the sketch was a start. "I'll get this circulating."

"Paige said she has a photo to show you," Corinna said. "She's still in the conference room."

"Thanks. If you can give me a few minutes,

I'll take you back to Gisella's," Ben said. "And we can go over the funeral arrangements."

She closed her eyes as if in pain. "Can we do that later tonight?" When she opened her eyes and stared at him he saw the plea in her pretty gaze. "I'm really not up for that right now. I'd rather go to the studio. I really need to rehearse. The benefit show is less than a week away."

He admired her dedication in the face of such grief. "Are you sure you're up to it?"

Some unidentifiable emotion flickered deep in her eyes. "I need to."

Respect for her courage filled him. He understood that need. Working the case was helping him to deal with his own sorrow. Dancing might help her heal. Or at least take her mind off her grief.

"Okay. I'll have an SAPD officer outside the studio at all times. You are not to go off anywhere alone," he said with a pointed look.

One corner of her mouth tipped upward in acknowledgement. "I can live with that. I've learned my lesson."

Satisfied, he led her from the office back to the conference room. Oliver had a hip hiked on the table near Paige.

Oliver straightened as they entered the room.

"Paige was just telling me you caught a glimpse of the guy who broke into your house last night."

Ben showed him the sketch. "I want every law enforcement officer within a hundred-mile radius to have a copy of this. We need to catch this guy."

Oliver studied the picture with a furrowed brow. "Sure, boss." He loped out of the conference room.

Paige stood and withdrew a photo from a large square leather case. "I took the liberty of enhancing the photo of the second shooting victim. Since our facial recognition software has been unsuccessful in identifying this man, I thought you might want to release his picture to the public."

Ben took the photo. It looked like coma guy, but in the rendering the man's eyes were open and his face clean shaven. "How do you know he has blue eyes?"

Paige arched an eyebrow. "I stopped by the hospital on the way in and took a peek. The imaging software on my laptop is top notch. It was easy to plug in coma guy's specs and come up with a nearly flawless image. Thankfully, you all have good quality printers here."

"Great job." Ben walked to the door and called out, "Anderson!"

A few seconds later, Anderson Michaels appeared in the doorway. He flashed the ladies a charming smile before addressing Ben. "You rang?"

Ben handed him the photo of coma guy. "See what you can do about getting this on the air. Hopefully, someone will come forward with some information."

"Sure thing, boss." Anderson took the photo.

Ben shook Paige's hand. "Thank you. You did good work today."

Paige gave him a friendly but sad smile. "I just hope we catch this perp."

"We'll walk out with you," Ben said. They all left the building together. Ben made sure Paige was on her way in her car before he started his Jeep. Corinna struggled with the passenger seat belt.

"Problem?" he asked.

"It's twisted," she muttered.

"Here, let me." He leaned over to reach for the top of the shoulder harness. His chest came in contact with her shoulder. Her breath fanned out over his neck; the scent of her orangey shampoo filled his senses. His gaze traveled over her face. The complexity of longing and frustration playing across her features fascinated him. He searched her warm brown eyes.

His breathing hitched as an answering longing hit the pit of his stomach and worked its way into the vicinity of his heart. His hand slid along the rough material of the shoulder strap, his fingers trailing inches from her body as he unwound the harness. He stopped at the buckle and secured the seat belt into place with a click.

And still he stayed in place, leaning close, maintaining the contact of his chest to her shoulder. He savored her scent and the way her mouth opened slightly as if she, too, was having as much trouble catching her breath as he was.

It would be so easy to dip his head and claim her mouth. Too easy to lose himself in the moment. Too easy to forget that she was Greg's daughter and way off-limits.

But not that easy.

He lurched away and gripped the steering wheel. He had to remember his promise. No matter how magnetic Corinna's draw was on him. Greg had counted on Ben to protect her. And that meant from himself, as well as the rest of the world.

SEVEN

As Ben drove through town, Corinna fought to regain control of her breathing. For a moment, she'd thought Ben was going to kiss her. Anticipation had thrummed through her system, setting her already taut nerves on high alert. But then he'd jerked back, leaving her feeling disappointed and irrational for even contemplating a kiss.

She glanced discreetly at his profile. His ruggedly handsome features were grim with concentration. More concentration than the afternoon traffic warranted. His big, strong hands gripped the wheel, turning his knuckles white as he drove through downtown San Antonio. Clearly, he was upset.

Because he'd wanted to kiss her?

The thought was heady, yet she had no business thinking of him in any romantic way. Only heartache lay down that road. He lived a life she wanted to leave behind her. A dangerous, unpredictable life. A life that took her father. She tugged the resentment and anger she'd been harboring for so long more securely in place and told herself to be grateful he'd had the self-control to put a stop to the attraction arcing between them. Her own willpower to resist him was in short supply. She could trust that Ben would stay true to his convictions.

She gave a mental scoff. Trust was definitely *not* one of her issues with Ben.

When he pulled the Jeep to the curb in front of the white, flat-roof building housing the San Antonio professional ballet company, she was out the door with her bag before he'd even turned off the engine. She needed the distance.

He exited and came around the front of the vehicle as an SAPD officer stepped from his cruiser parked nearby. She paused on the walkway as Ben and the officer caught up to her.

The two men shook hands.

"I've secured the premises. The only other exit besides the front door has an alarm. I've also cautioned the staff to keep all the windows locked."

"I appreciate that," Ben said. He turned to Corinna. "This is Officer Hagerty."

She nodded a greeting to the older gentleman. "Officer."

"Miss Pike, I'm sorry for your loss. Your father was a good man," Officer Hagerty said. His deep voice echoed with sincerity.

Sadness bowed her shoulders. She could only give him a lackluster smile. Clutching her bag to her chest, she turned to go, but Ben's hand on her arm halted her progress.

"What time should I pick you up?" Ben asked.

The last thing she wanted was to spend more time alone with him. He unsettled her, made her aware of her grief and loneliness, made her want things that could never be. "You don't need to be my chauffeur."

Surprise flickered in his gaze. "I don't mind. It's part of my job."

A shaft of anger pierced her. Disconcerted, she said roughly, "I'd rather you concentrated on the part of your job that brings my father's murderer to justice."

A pained expression crossed his features.

Her cheeks stung with contrition for lashing out. She took a deep breath before adding in a more careful tone, "I'm sure Officer Hagerty could give me a ride to Gisella's when I'm ready to leave."

"Would be my pleasure," the officer replied.

Ben's eyebrows drew slightly together. She felt his gaze all the way to her toes. She fidgeted with her bag and couldn't help returning the favor of staring back.

Finally, he said, "I suppose Officer Hagerty driving you would be okay. Though I was thinking you might want to see Gabby tonight."

She did miss the feline and could really use a dose of her unconditional love. But that would mean not only more time with Ben, but going to his apartment again. She wasn't sure that was a good idea. Being too close, too alone with him made her ache with yearnings that had no business invading her life. She didn't want to get attached, caught up in his world. The same world had taken her father from her.

She had to clear her throat of the yearning before she could answer. "I can see her tomorrow. You mentioned getting me a key."

"I did. I'll have one made tonight and bring it by tomorrow morning."

Why did he keep suggesting they see each other? He couldn't possibly know she was having trouble keeping her heart from wanting him.

Flustered, she stumbled back a step toward the door. "You can just give it to Gisella."

He blinked. "Okay. If that's what you want."

"It is." She backed up another step, creating more space between them. "I need to go."

Ben's lips pressed together in a firm line.

She turned and hurried inside before she could give into the urge to soothe away his upset. She hoped the next time she heard from Ben he'd tell her he'd found her father's killer, even though logically, she knew it could take months for that to happen. But that was all she wanted from him. Wasn't it?

After dropping Corinna off at the studio and making sure the officer there was aware of the danger to Corinna's life, Ben headed back to the Ranger headquarters. He had work to do on Greg's case, but his mind kept wandering to her. As breakable as she appeared, he kept catching glimpses of a core of steel.

Over the last few days he'd become aware of her on a deep, visceral level and that scared him. He wanted to distance himself, yet at every turn he found himself drawing closer to this complicated and fascinating woman.

The fact that she'd made her feelings clear, that

she didn't want anything to do with him, should make him happy. But he wasn't.

He'd been around her numerous times over the years, but he'd never really gotten to know her. Partly because of the age difference—seven years had seemed a huge spread when he was nineteen and she was twelve. As adults, the years didn't seem like much.

Except the main reason he'd never had the chance to know her was Greg. From the very first, Greg had warned Ben off, saying, "Remember, she's my daughter. Show her respect."

Ben had heard the underlying message in those words loud and clear over the years, each time Greg repeated the refrain. *Stay away. Off-limits. You're not good enough for her.*

He blew out a harsh breath. Yeah, he accepted Greg had wanted more for his daughter. A life untouched by the evil they dealt with. Getting involved with a Ranger would keep her tied to that world.

Come on, he had to get a grip, had to stop thinking about her and concentrate on finding the murderer before he got to Corinna. Because only then would he be able to move forward with his life as captain of Company D.

* * *

"Here's a good one," Corinna said, handing a picture of her parents over to Ben for his perusal. They sat at the kitchen table in her family home. The evening sun had begun to set on another endless day. Tomorrow would be the funeral. Corinna couldn't believe three days had passed since her father's death. They seemed like a lifetime. She'd been shot at, she'd shot at someone and then presumably the same guy tried to break into the room where she was sleeping. It was a lot to take in.

Her hand shook slightly, making the photo waver. She was struggling to maintain her self-control as they pored over pictures chronologically of her father's life for the montage to be displayed at the memorial.

"I see where you get your beauty," Ben murmured as he gazed at the picture of her parents when they were newly married.

She appreciated his compliment but her emotions were scraped raw; all she could muster was a brief smile in acknowledgment.

The board where Ben tacked the pictures was nearly full. Corinna bit her lip to keep her tears from flowing. It just wasn't right. Her father shouldn't be dead. Her fists clenched. *Why? Why?* her mind silently screamed.

"This is great," Ben said, taking a photo out of another box and holding it up for her to see. "We have to use this."

Her breath caught.

The image showed her father from the chest up, holding a small baby in his big, strong hands. The look of tender love on his handsome face was her undoing. Corinna could no longer hold back the tears. She pushed away from the table and ran out the back patio door.

Ben came out behind her, but she kept running all the way to the horse pasture. Thankfully her neighbor had agreed to care for the animals. As she neared the fence, one of the stallions trotted over. A big roan Quarter Horse named Dasher. She climbed the planks and allowed the animal to nuzzle her neck as she wrapped her arms around his head. Tears flowed, running down her cheeks to dampen the horse's satin coat.

She heard Ben approach and quickly dried her eyes. She felt the horse growing wary at the stranger. It occurred to her that Ben never visited the horses when he came to their house. A safe enough subject for now. She lifted her head to see him standing back a few feet. "You don't like horses?"

He met her gaze. "Not particularly. I ride when I have to."

He meant in parades and such, which was sometimes required of the Rangers. "Did something happen to spook you?"

"No. They're just really big animals and unpredictable."

"And you like things predictable."

"I like things I can control," he countered.

She stroked Dasher's neck. "Horses are controllable. You just have to know how to gain their trust."

"A lot like people," he said.

"I suppose." She stared off into the distance. The flat terrain of the sprawling state lay in darkness now that the sun had finished setting. Though a quarter moon rose, it didn't provide enough light to illuminate the land. Everything seemed to be in shadows. Just like her life. "I guess I'll have to sell this place."

Her father had loved this land, this ranch. She couldn't imagine someone else living here.

"Not until you're ready." Ben's answer was quick and decisive.

She nodded. Impulsively she said, "I want the memorial here, not at the funeral home."

"But all the arrangements have been made," he protested, his voice closer now. "Besides, it would be too dangerous having people coming and going from the house. It'd be too easy for a bad guy to sneak in among the guests."

"I don't care. I want it here. If a bad guy does sneak in, you and the other Rangers will be here to take him down." She glanced over her shoulder at him, but could barely make out his features in the dim glow of the moon. "Please. It's important to me. I don't want the memorial in some unfamiliar, sterile place. Can you make it happen?"

His voice softened. "If that's what you want."

"It is." She reached for one last stroke of Dasher's smooth cheek before hopping off the fence. She nearly knocked Ben over. He was closer than she'd thought. His strong hands steadied her. His masculine scent mingled with the smells of the hay and horse, making a heady, potent combination. Her mouth went dry. Unfamiliar yearnings spiked. She longed for Ben's arms to slide around her, for him to press her close and tell her everything was going to be all right.

And the world tilted slightly.

She swayed. Ben tightened his hold. "Corinna,

maybe you should come inside and have a drink of water."

Gathering her equilibrium and sanity, she pulled out of his grasp. The last thing she needed was to be attracted to or attached to Ben. He was part of her father's world. A place she had every intention of leaving behind. "I think I should return to Gisella's now."

She needed to go somewhere, anywhere away from him and the confusing sensations swirling around her head and chipping away at her heart.

Ben stood at the graveside of his fallen captain. The casket hovered over an open pit lined with a red velvet covering. The red, white and blue flag draped over the polished mahogany-wood casket fluttered in the humid breeze. The pastor gave the eulogy in soothing modulated tones. The faint sound of crying lifted on a puff of air.

The blustery fall day, heavy with humidity and rain, had been predicted. Wearing his best navy suit, Ben barely noticed the temperature as his gaze searched through the throng of mourners gathered in the Sunset Memorial Park cemetery. He hoped that the murderer would give him or herself away. But so far no one raised an alarm in Ben's senses. No one in the crowd resembled the intruder in the sketch.

There was a handful of civilians in attendance, all of whom had been checked out by the Rangers. Neighbors, buddies from Greg's college days, family friends from when the late Mrs. Pike had been alive.

The majority of those present were in law enforcement and Ben's mind rebelled at the thought of any of these men and women being in cahoots with Greg's murderer. Still, Ben tried to view each with a critical eye.

Sheriff Layton, in full dress uniform, his shocking white hair blowing in the wind, stood with his arm around his petite wife. Grief cut deep lines in his craggy face. A good number of San Antonio police officers in dress uniform were also in attendance.

Senior Captain Parker and his wife, a willowy red-head, held hands, their expressions somber. Beside them stood Ranger Assistant Chief Ambrose Ralston, a heavy-set man with a normally jolly disposition. Today he appeared grim as he paid his respects. Sweat beaded on his flaccid face.

Behind and flanking the chiefs stood a sea of white-hatted, dark-suited, silver-starred Rangers, from all the companies around the state. The loss of one of their own reflected in each face.

Ben's gaze roamed over the more prestigious mourners. The death of a Ranger deserved the respect of every office of the state, including its official representatives. San Antonio Mayor Les Bernard, in his mid-forties with sandy blond hair and GQ looks in a well-tailored suit, stood with his platinum blonde wife, but there was a gap of space between them.

Texas State Senator Frederick Huffington, in his late fifties and decidedly on the paunchy side in a brown suit stood staring at the casket. At his side, his spouse dabbed at her nose with a tissue.

And finally, the head of the State of Texas, Governor John Kingston, a regal man in his late sixties in a pin-striped suit, held an arm firmly around his silver-haired wife.

All were properly solemn. No inkling that any had wished Captain Pike ill. Not that Ben had expected to see ill will among the prominent attendees. The murder was related to whatever case Greg had been working.

His gaze sought Corinna. She stood sandwiched between the senator and the governor, teary-eyed, sad and heartbreakingly beautiful. Her sleeveless black knee-length dress almost dwarfed her. The wound on her arm was covered with a flesh-colored bandage. His stomach muscles contracted every time he saw the reminder of how close she'd come to death.

A little black hat with a mesh veil covered her slicked-back hair. Her oval-shaped, pale face stood out in stark contrast. But it was her eyes, so bleak, so full of pain each time she glanced around her, that grabbed Ben by the gut and squeezed tight.

For days he'd ached for her loss and the pain she was trying to control. Even knowing she was well-guarded hadn't eased the tightness in his chest. Nor had helping her plan the funeral. Seeing her distress had only cut him deeper.

Knowing she was so full of anger at God hurt him to the core. He'd prayed long and hard for God to comfort her and give her peace. And he prayed God would answer the question. Not the one asking why God had allowed this to happen, but rather who had killed Greg, and why.

Frustratingly, the Rangers' investigation seemed to be at a dead end. The DA hadn't found a link between Greg's death and any old cases he'd worked. Forensics hadn't revealed anything useful; the facial recognition software had yet to give names to their unconscious victim or the intruder whom Corinna had seen. Ben wasn't any closer to knowing what Greg had been working on.

Aggravation and anger revved through him every time he realized that if they didn't get a break soon, the person who'd killed Greg was going to get away with it.

Ben clenched his jaw and vowed never to stop investigating Greg's death. No matter how long the search for the killer took.

The melancholy sound of a flute playing "Amazing Grace" pulled Ben from his thoughts. He and Daniel stepped forward to carefully remove the American flag from the coffin and fold it into a triangle. Ben presented the folded flag to Corinna. Her delicate hands closed over his for a moment. Her skin was icy and sent a shiver of awareness up Ben's arm. Their gazes met. Ben felt her grief down to the marrow of his bones.

He inclined his head, acknowledging their shared pain, and released his hold. Corinna clutched the flag to her chest and closed her eyes. Tears slipped down her cheeks. Ben positioned himself at her side and encircled her waist with his arm. She stiffened but didn't move away. One by one the mourners paraded in front of her, offering murmured condolences before leaving the grave site.

When only the Rangers of Company D remained, Ben led Corinna toward the waiting limousine that would take them back to the Pike house, where Corinna had insisted the mourners gather for a memorial service.

Once inside the roomy car, Corinna settled on the leather seat with a sigh. "I hate this."

Sitting across from her, Ben leaned forward to take her cold hands in his and rubbed them in an effort to warm her up. "You're doing great."

She gave him a wan smile that didn't reach her eyes. "It was nice to see so many people had cared for my father."

"He was well-loved and respected."

One side of her mouth lifted in a cynical smile. "So it would seem. But someone out there didn't love him. Someone killed him. I searched every face in the crowd for someone who looked guilty, who seemed satisfied to see my father in the grave. I came up empty. The guy in the sketch wasn't there, either." She pinned him with an intense look. "Do you think the guy that broke in is the same person who killed my father?"

"I won't know until we catch him."

She turned to stare out the window. "What if he's not? What if there's someone else behind Dad's murder?"

"Then we keep pushing for the truth."

"But maybe at the house someone will slip up and we can nail the person responsible for my father's death."

Her words slammed into his gut. Now he understood why she'd wanted the service to be at her house. She hoped to trap a killer. Concern pounded in his veins.

His own disappointment that he hadn't brought the murderer down yet coiled inside of him. Rage smoldered like a burning coal left in the grate. He could only do so much with the little bit of evidence they had. And it wasn't enough. His jaw tightened. Failure wasn't an option. Not on this.

And Corinna's safety was paramount.

"You need to leave the investigation to me."

"I'm my father's daughter," she said, her dark eyes hard in a way he'd never seen. "I will do my part to help bring this murderer to justice."

"And put yourself in danger again? No way!"

She narrowed her gaze. "I'll do what I have to."

Extracting her hands, she faced toward the

side window, creating a chasm of grief and anger between them as wide as the Rio Grande.

Taken aback by the stubborn streak he'd never noticed before, a knot of dread formed in his chest. He wished he could do something, say anything to ease her pain and make her see that what she was suggesting was foolhardy. But he came up empty. He understood the desire to bring down whoever did this, but it was his job, not hers.

His duty was to protect her, as well as find a murderer. But the truth was, he had nothing to go on. And no way to bridge the distance between them.

Why did that bother him so much?

The limo halted in the driveway. Corinna needed to get out of the suffocating car. Without waiting for anyone to open the door, she grabbed the handle, pushed the door wide and climbed out. For a moment, memories of the awful night when she'd found her father dead threatened to swamp her, but she forced her feet to move toward the front door of her home.

She entered the house and paused. A strange sense of unease slithered across her flesh. Soon guests would be arriving and one of them just might be the killer.

Noises coming from the kitchen sent her heart pounding. Oh, how she wished it was her father cooking one of his special meals. Melancholy enveloped her with the same weight as a heavy blanket. He would never be in the kitchen again. A reality she hated, but had to face.

Knowing she had to keep busy if she was going to make it through the next few hours as her house filled with people, she hurried toward the kitchen in search of something to do. Gisella and Marissa were helping the caterer put out a huge spread of food ranging from triangle sandwiches to stuffed mushrooms and shrimp cocktails.

"What can I do?" Corinna asked as she stepped up to the counter separating the kitchen from the dining area.

"Nothing," Marissa said. "You relax. We've got everything under control."

"There must be something," Corinna insisted, her gaze meeting Gisella's.

Gisella wiped her hands on a towel and then came around the counter to give Corinna a quick hug. In the short span of time that Corinna had come to know Gisella, they'd become tentative friends. Gisella seemed to understand Corinna in a way few others did.

When Gisella stepped back, she gestured toward the dining table where several trays of hors d'oeuvres were laid out. "You can take a plate of appetizers to the living room."

Grateful for the task, Corinna grabbed a tray of pastry puffs filled with crab and headed into the living area. The room rapidly filled. There were a few of her fellow dancers who'd come to pay their respects. Madame Martin, the director of the San Antonio Ballet Company pulled her close for a quick hug of sympathy. Annie Nelson, the founder of Miriam's Shelter also offered her condolences.

But the Rangers of Company D, many of whom had been here the night her father died, gave her a measure of comfort. She knew they would work tirelessly to find their captain's killer.

She swallowed hard and tried to put on a good face as people offered their sympathies. She couldn't even look at the picture board set up in the living room on an easel. Bringing out the photos had been difficult enough.

When the conversation turned to stories of her father, Corinna's chest constricted until she could hardly breathe. These people knew a different side of her father. A side that he'd kept from her.

At home when they were alone, he'd been like a big teddy bear, catering to his only child's needs. She cherished those times together, just her and her father. But he was different when Ben was around, more rough and gruff. More guyish. Excluding her from their activities, making her feel displaced and alone.

And on the job, from the stories the Rangers told, there was yet another side to him. Captain Pike was an intimidating man who got the job done regardless of the risk.

She wished she'd known that Greg Pike, too. She would have liked to see her father in action. But he'd kept her far away from his job, always saying his work was no place for his ballerina. The ghost of the need to impress her father with her tomboy shenanigans cast a shadow over her heart as it passed through her.

Her gaze strayed to Ben. A man cut from the same cloth as her father? Of course he was. Her father had handpicked him to be the surrogate son he'd always wanted. Trained him to be a Ranger. A captain. Groomed him to be his replacement. The knot in her chest tightened more. Her breathing grew labored, as if she couldn't quite take in enough oxygen.

Corinna quietly slipped out of the room and retreated to the back patio. The late afternoon sun was low in the sky. The wind had died down, leaving the air heavy and damp. In the distance, Corinna heard the whinny of the horses in the pasture. They missed her father, too.

A swift, unrelenting misery pelted her, the ache so acute she doubled over, wrapping one arm around her middle while her other hand groped for something to hold on to.

Then Ben was there. A solid wall of muscular chest and gentle hands descending on her shoulders.

"Corinna, honey. Oh, man," he said in a emotion-laden voice. "Come here."

He pulled her tightly against him, his familiar scent of spice and masculinity filling her head.

Everything inside of her wanted to lash out, to beat her fists against him, to rail at him for being the son her father wanted.

Instead she clung to him, needing him to anchor her, to keep her from spiraling down a rabbit hole of despair and anguish. A sob escaped from that weak place in her.

"I know. I know. I miss him, too." He made soft murmuring, comforting noises that stirred her senses. One big, strong hand smoothed over her back. The rhythmic motion caused a maelstrom of sensation to burst through her, taking her by surprise.

For the past few days she'd felt only the sorrow and loss of her father. She'd become numb to anything else. But now...

She titled her head to gaze up into Ben's handsome face. His jaw was so strong and stubborn. He'd removed his hat, giving her a better view of his eyes; warm hazel eyes reflecting her pain. His gaze was as tender as a caress, touching on her face, her lips. His mouth was so close, beckoning her.

Without giving herself time to think, to hold back, she rose on tiptoe and placed her lips against his. He jerked in surprise before his firm mouth yielded. He took what she offered and gave what she needed. He pressed her closer as she dragged her hands through his hair, concentrating on the feel of the short strands gliding over her palms.

A deep sense of peace, of rightness, seeped into her, chasing away the searing pain. She savored the connection, needing to feel, something, anything besides sorrow.

Abruptly, Ben wrenched his mouth from her. His breathing came in ragged puffs. He blinked as horror chased the tenderness from his eyes. He set her away from him.

"This is wrong. I'm so sorry," he said, his voice full of self-recrimination. "I shouldn't have done that. You're grieving and vulnerable right now. This… I can't… Please, forgive me."

Confusion and humiliation burned her cheeks. Why had she crossed such a critical line? No good had come from giving in to her need for connection.

She turned and fled back into the house.

With the memorial over and the Rangers no closer to knowing who had killed her father, Corinna sat curled on her bed at Gisella's staring at the shadows playing across her wall. The house was too still, too lonely. Even with Gisella just down the hall.

Corinna's heart hurt.

It was awful enough her dad was gone, but on top of everything she'd made a fool of herself with Ben.

After the embarrassing encounter on the patio, she'd felt his gaze following her the rest of the afternoon, but she couldn't meet his eyes.

What she'd done, reaching out for comfort—and that's all she'd been doing—had been a mistake.

She had to find a way to deal with her crumbling world without looking to Ben for help.

It didn't matter that they shared the bond of grief.

Ben was not the man for her.

And she'd do best to remember that.

EIGHT

Flipping open the top file of the stack he had brought from the Pike house, Ben stared unseeingly for several long moments, his mind running back over the events from the memorial service. Or rather the one event out on the patio with Corinna.

His mind flashed to the kiss they'd shared. She'd surprised him when she'd initiated the contact. And he'd surprised himself by giving himself over to her touch and being swamped by a yearning for connection.

Self-recriminations jabbed at him. How could he dishonor his friend and mentor by taking advantage of his grieving daughter?

The sooner he found the murderer and eliminated the threat to Corinna, the better for them all. Because he wasn't sure he could continue to protect her so closely and resist the need to kiss her again.

He forced himself to scan the pages of the file looking for some hint of what Greg had been working on before he died. He reached the end of the file. Nothing.

Three files later, Ben finally found something odd. A random sticky note with the words *Lions of Texas* written across the top in Greg's bold handwriting.

Ben had never heard the term before and he couldn't connect the reference to anything even after carefully perusing the file's contents. The file was an old murder case long solved with the criminal in jail. Why would Greg write this note and leave it in the folder?

Ben called the San Antonio prison and talked with the warden. The criminal convicted of murder and serving three life sentences had died the year before. He'd been rumored to be part of a Mexican Mafia prison gang by the name of La Eme. The warden had never heard of the Lions of Texas.

Frustrated, Ben hung up. An Internet search also came up empty. His phone rang. The administrative assistant, Marissa, put through a call from Senior Captain Parker.

"Fritz here," Ben said into the receiver.

"Good morning, Captain." Senior Captain Parker's voice filled the line. "I trust you're settling into your new role?"

Ben's gaze drifted to the filing cabinet. Sitting in prominent view on top was a group photo of Company D taken the year before. Greg stood in the center, flanked by the Rangers. Sorrow weighed heavy on his shoulders. He missed Greg.

"Trying, sir."

"Are you any closer to finding Greg's killer?" Captain Parker asked.

As if his own expectations weren't already knotted in his gut, pressure from everyone else's expectations built in his chest. He related the events of the last few days. He could still feel the surge of fear that had hit him when he'd first received Corinna's call. If something had happened to her…

"And you think this man who broke into the Pike house and later tried to break into Ranger Hernandez's house is the same man who shot Greg?"

Ben wasn't sure of anything. "I can only assume so until I have proof otherwise."

"Keep me informed."

"I will, sir." He fingered the sticky note. "Have you heard of the Lions of Texas?"

"Hmm. Can't say that I have." Curiosity echoed in his tone. "What are they?"

Ben stared at the boldly written words. "Not sure. I found a reference in a closed-case file."

"That's interesting. I'll ask around."

"I'd appreciate it, sir."

Parker cleared his throat. "The reason I called… as you know this coming March marks the 175th anniversary of the Battle of the Alamo. The governor himself requested that the Texas Rangers of Company D take a more active role in this year's special celebration."

For a shocked moment, Ben couldn't speak as the request sank in. Shaking his head, he said, "Sir, with all due respect, we have more pressing matters at hand."

"Yes, you do. Finding Pike's killer is of the utmost importance. But so is the anniversary of the most significant event in Texas history. Company D is the San Antonio branch of the Rangers, and as such, the Alamo is your territory." The deep timbre of his voice dared Ben to challenge his mandate.

Ben couldn't refute that claim. The Battle of the Alamo symbolized courage and sacrifice for the cause of liberty. The liberty the Rangers worked tirelessly to uphold. Ben's gaze again looked to the picture of Greg.

He would want them to honor their state with their service in the celebration. Greg had been big on keeping traditions alive. "What exactly will be required?"

"For now, the time involved should be minimal. I'm sure the planning committee will have all the details laid out."

That was something at least. "Very well, sir."

"Connect me back to Marissa, and I'll leave the celebration committee's contact info with her," Parker said.

Ben transferred the call to his administrative assistant, wondering how his team would react to this new assignment.

Twenty minutes later, after Marissa gave him the meeting information with the Alamo committee, Ben had the Rangers gathered together in the conference room. He told them about the Alamo celebration and the request for their presence.

"You've got to be kidding me." Marvel said. "I, for one, am not in the mood for any sort of celebrating. Not until we bring Captain Pike's murderer to justice."

There were murmured agreements around the room.

Ben held up a hand. "I understand, believe me, but we will do this in honor of our fallen captain. Greg would have relished this kind of opportunity to show the public who and what we are. This won't take place for six months. We'll have found Greg's killer by then," he said, hoping his optimism wasn't misplaced.

"Do we know what this 'presence' will entail?" Cade asked.

"At this point, no. Anderson and Daniel, I want you to meet with the committee. Once we have a better idea of what's involved, I'll let the rest of you know."

"When is this meeting?" Daniel asked.

"Tomorrow morning."

Trevor shifted in his seat. "Why them?"

Ben didn't really feel the need to explain himself, but in the name of keeping the peace, he bit back a sharp retort and said, "Daniel's late father moved in the same circle as many of the committee members so they already know and trust him and Anderson's good with people. I think they are the best choice to be the intermediaries between the Rangers and the committee. Is there a problem?"

Trevor's lip curled but he didn't respond.

Ben held up the square notepaper. "I found something unusual. Anyone heard of the Lions of Texas?"

No one had.

"What are they?" Gisella asked.

"I don't know. The file I found this tucked inside was a closed murder case from about six years ago. The perp went to prison, where he died. The warden said he'd been part of La Eme."

"Nasty business, that," Evan Chen said. "Mexican Mafia. They're a prison gang that started in the '50s in California. They've grown and spread across the country. Rival gangs have sprouted up over the years in response, as well."

Ben appreciated Evan's input. The Ranger had been a narcotics officer with the Dallas police force before coming to the Rangers. "So this Lions of Texas could be a new prison gang?"

Evan shrugged. "If so, the Feds would have info on them."

"Good idea," Ben said. "Can you contact our local Feds to see what you can find out about the Lions of Texas and if there is a connection to La Eme?"

"I can."

"Anderson, where are we on getting coma guy's picture to the media?"

He pushed away from the wall where he'd been leaning. "Should be on the eleven o'clock news again tonight, along with a sketch of the intruder."

Ben nodded with approval. "Perfect. Hopefully, someone will come forward with an ID. Oliver, you got that sketch sent out?"

Oliver stretched back in his seat. "Yep. Every police and Ranger station in the state has a copy. It's only a matter of waiting until we get a hit."

Ben tried not to give any ground to the impatience hovering at the periphery of his consciousness. Waiting was part of the game. But patience wasn't one of his stronger virtues.

Instead, he sent up a silent plea for God to allow someone to recognize both of the mystery men so he could find Greg's murderer, remove any danger to Corinna and put this case to rest.

Then Ben could stop thinking—make that *worrying*—about Corinna.

The next day, Ben found Corinna surrounded by a dozen little girls all dressed in pink frills at Miriam's Shelter, an old, ranch-style house on the outskirts of San Antonio.

He'd heard music and had followed the sound to the open side door of the garage where he now stood in the shadows. A makeshift dance studio had been set up in the tandem garage. Wood flooring had been put down across the cement and two free-standing ballet bars ran lengthwise. Mirrors covered the back of the garage from floor to ceiling. A soft, trilling melody played from a stereo system in the corner.

He watched fascinated as Corinna patiently taught her little charges, helping to position a foot here, straightening an arm there. Her smile was tender, transforming her face from beautiful to exquisite.

He swallowed hard, reining in the attraction as affection blossomed inside. He was here to check on her, not gawk at her like some lovestruck teen.

One of the little girls, a blue-eyed, blonde cherub with riotous curls framing her dimpled face, met his gaze. For a moment, the child froze, then terror flashed in those sweet eyes. She let out a shrill screech that could have torn paint off the walls.

Corinna acted swiftly, swooping the child up and gathering the rest close. A door leading to the main part of the shelter jerked open and a husky woman of about fifty burst out, a shotgun in hand. In two blinks she had the gun aimed at his chest. Several other women rushed out and moved to shield the children.

Stepping into the light, Ben raised his hands, hoping the woman didn't have twitchy fingers. "Whoa, there. Ranger Fritz here." He gestured to his badge pinned to the breast pocket of his button-down shirt.

"Ben!" Corinna's voice carried over the crying girls. "What on earth are you doing?"

"I came to check on you. Can you please ask your friend to lower the gun?"

"It's okay, Annie. He's a friend." Corinna disengaged herself from the children.

Annie's gaze held suspicion. "Are you sure?"

Corinna put her hand on the older woman's arm. "I'm sure. He and my father were very close."

The gun lowered. "Oh, well, in that case."

Ben let out a sigh of relief. "Sorry to have upset everyone." His gaze held Corinna's. "I didn't intend to interrupt."

She came forward and took his hand. Tugging him closer to the huddled group, she said, "Everyone, this is Captain Ben Fritz, a Texas Ranger. He's a good guy. Like the police officer outside." She touched the badge on his chest. "If you ever see a man wearing one of these, you can be assured he's a good guy."

Though there was still suspicion in the eyes of the adult women, the children relaxed. A few even seemed curious.

The tiny angel with the big lungs came forward. "What ya doing here?"

Ben knelt down at her eye level. "I came to see my friend Corinna. What's your name?"

"Gretchen."

He held out his hand. "Hello, Miss Gretchen."

The child hesitated before slipping her small hand into his. "Hello."

Ben released her hand and gestured with his head toward Corinna. "She's a good teacher, isn't she?"

The blond head bobbed. "She sure is. And she bought us all our tutus." The girl proudly displayed her pink outfit.

"You look just like a fairy princess. All you need are some glittery wings."

She giggled. "And a tiara."

He slapped his hand against his forehead. "How could I forget the tiara?"

"Look, I can peer-row-wet," Gretchen said and pivoted on her tiny slippered foot.

Ben gave a low whistle. "That's pretty special."

His gaze sought Corinna's. The gentle look in her eyes hit him square in the chest and made his heart speed up.

Corinna broke the eye contact and clapped her hands. "Okay, students. We'll end our lesson for today."

There were groans and protests from the children as the women ushered them inside the house.

Annie shot him one last appraising glare before saying to Corinna, "You need me, you just holler."

"I will," Corinna said with an amused lilt in her tone.

When they were alone, Ben said, "I'm sorry to have caused such a ruckus."

Corinna walked to the stereo, removed a CD and tucked it in her bag. "Usually, if a man shows up here, it doesn't go well. Some of the husbands or boyfriends of these women can get pretty mean."

"I can imagine." He frowned. "I'm not sure you being here is a good idea. Even with Officer Hagerty outside."

"I have to keep living, Ben." She picked up her dance bag and walked toward him. "Now, I'm off to the studio. Was there something you needed? Did someone recognize the guy in the sketch?"

"Not yet, but it's only been a couple of days." There was a reason he'd come to see her—one that had to do with the investigation. But he couldn't tell her the other reason—that he missed her. "Had you ever heard your father mention the Lions of Texas?"

She shook her head as she preceded him out the side door into the side yard. "Doesn't sound familiar. What is it?"

He blew out an exasperated breath. "I wish I knew. I found those words written on a sticky note in a random file. Can't seem to find the significance. Maybe there isn't one."

When they reached the front driveway, she paused to look up at him. "If it has something to do with my father's death, I trust you'll figure it out."

Her confidence made him feel like he could leap buildings in a single bound. Hmm. He'd never compared himself to a comic-book hero before. He sure didn't want to disappoint her. Or the others counting on him to get the job done. Pressure tensed his shoulders.

She laid a hand on his arm. Her touch sent ribbons of longing through him. Again he wondered where this attraction to her had come from? And how was he supposed to ignore it?

"You don't have to keep checking up on me. It makes me feel like you don't trust me," she said.

"It's not you I don't trust," he replied, putting his feelings into his voice. "It's everyone else."

"Not even the Rangers?"

Contrition lifted one corner of his mouth. "Okay, them I trust."

She arched an eyebrow. "And SAPD?"

He barked out a short laugh. "All right. I get it. You don't want me hovering."

"No, I don't." She removed her hand and backed away. "I'm okay without you."

Her words carved into him as neatly as a butterfly knife does a freshly caught trout. Gathering his composure, he saluted her. "No worries. I won't bother you again."

He resolved to keep his promise—from a distance. It was safer that way.

Over the next couple of days, Ben dealt with seven cases that crossed his desk. He'd delegated each to a Ranger so he could concentrate on finding Greg's murderer and keeping Corinna safe from the man who wanted to prevent her from identifying him.

Now, he tried to contain his mounting aggravation as he finished reading Evan's report from the Feds. They hadn't heard of the Lions of Texas either, but promised to check with their informants within the penal system to see if this was a new gang.

Coma guy was still unconscious. So far every avenue of identifying him had come up empty. How could the guy be so completely off the grid?

And the sketch of the man who'd broken into Corinna's house hadn't garnered any hits either. Frustration had become Ben's constant companion.

Gisella knocked on Ben's office door. Grateful for a distraction, he waved her in. She strode inside and took a seat across from the desk.

"I'm worried about Corinna," she said without pre-amble.

The mention of Corinna's name tightened something inside Ben's chest. Though he'd had regular reports from Officer Hagerty and was assured she was safe at all times, Ben had had to fight the urge to see for himself. She'd asked him not to and he was honoring that request.

Every night when he went home he found subtle clues she'd been there visiting Gabby. A couch pillow out of place, the cat's dishes filled. Corinna's scent, fresh and fruity, lingering in the air.

And now here was Gisella saying she was worried about Corinna. Apprehension lanced through him. "What's happened?"

Gisella held up her hand. "Nothing. She's fine. No more break-in attempts. It's…it's just she's pushing herself so hard. She hardly eats, hardly sleeps. She's at the dance studio for hours without a break. Then at the shelter. I know she has this thing coming up, but all this coming and going exposes her. And I'm afraid she's going to wear herself out."

Concern burned through him. Honoring Corinna's request to stay away worked only if she remained okay. But from the sounds of it she really wasn't. "I'll talk to her."

"I know Greg would have appreciated that," Gisella said, her dark eyes sad. "I can only imagine how hard this must be for her."

Ben cleared his throat to relieve the choking grief welling up. "Yes. For all of us."

Levi appeared in the doorway. Energy emanated from his muscular frame. "Hey, just got a call.

There's been a bank heist downtown. It's turned into a hostage situation. Local PD has requested help."

Adrenaline crashed through Ben in a wave. He jumped up, ready to go. But then he remembered. He was captain. His job was to delegate and coordinate. Staying would be hard but necessary. "Go, both of you. Take Oliver and Trevor."

Gisella rushed out after Levi, leaving Ben alone. Slowly he resumed his seat, confident in his team's abilities.

His team.

A pang of sorrow robbed him of the pride he should be feeling.

His gaze sought the picture of Greg with the Rangers. "I'll do you proud," he whispered.

NINE

When Ben arrived a little after eight in the evening at the San Antonio Ballet Company, he found Officer Hagerty standing guard outside one of the studio doors. A haunting melody wafted from the other side of the door. The rest of the building was dark and quiet.

"Is she alone?" Ben asked.

Hagerty nodded. "Everyone else left an hour ago. She usually stays an extra hour."

Reaching for the door handle, Ben said, "I'll take her home tonight."

Hagerty inclined his head. "Appreciate it." The officer ambled out. A few seconds later, his police cruiser left the parking lot.

Ben eased open the door and stepped inside the hardwood-floored room. Mirrors covered the opposite wall from floor to ceiling, bisected by the wooden bar bolted into the glass. Classical music played on an iPod attached to an iHome. But it was the woman in the center of the room who held Ben enthralled.

He'd never seen Corinna dance. Her lithe form moved with grace, beauty and a frenetic energy as she twirled and spun, leapt and dipped. The graceful chaotic dance was almost painful to watch, yet Ben couldn't look away.

Her white leotard accentuated her thin and muscular frame, yet highlighted her curves. A fluttery skirt around her waist made her appear like an ethereal fairy, who might disappear at any moment. Her dark hair captured at her nape by a pink net served to draw his gaze to her swan-like neck. Her eyes were closed in her pale, oval-shaped face as she moved in tempo to the poignant tune.

The whole effect touched something deep inside Ben. Not quite sadness, not quite joy. Something unfamiliar welled in his chest, making his heart ache.

When he noticed tears slipping from beneath her long, dark lashes, the need to take her in his arms became unbearable.

He had to do something.

He moved forward, the heels of his suede boots making barely audible clicks on the gleaming hardwood floor. He stepped into her path as she spun toward him. She collided with his chest. His arm encircled her, harnessing her frenzied energy. She gave a startled yelp.

Her eyelids flew open. Panic fled and was replaced by recognition tempered with anguish and torment swirling in the depths of her gaze. Ben felt the impact of her sorrow deep in his soul.

Her breath came out in ragged puffs. She tried to wrench free. He held her, gently tightening his hold. She brought her small fist up to beat at his chest. He absorbed the blows, allowing her to let loose without restraint.

The blows tapered off and she dropped her head against his chest. He pulled her closer. Her arms encircled his waist as she let loose with big gulping sobs. Though he'd held her like this once before, there was something much more profound about this moment. Maybe it was the realization of just what their lives would be like with Greg gone.

He'd thought he was cried out, but as he rested his cheek against the top of her head, his own tears of grief freely flowed.

She quieted, pressing her cheek against his heart, sending warmth flooding his system. Her hands moved up his back, to his arms as she eased away to stare into his face. Her delicate features reminded him of a porcelain doll he'd once seen. Perfect, beautiful.

Her eyes darkened more as her hand reached behind his head and pulled him to her. He couldn't have resisted even if the thought had formed.

Their lips met, at once urgent and comforting. Sensation ran rampant through him. Yearning for a closeness he'd never experienced rose within him.

This went beyond the physical, to a heart level where a need for intimacy that had nothing to do with the kiss and everything to do with healing exploded. But true healing couldn't be found in a kiss. True healing came only from love. From God.

"Corinna," he murmured against her lips. "We can't."

"Shh," she pleaded, refusing to let him ease away. "Please, just hold me."

Everything inside of him wanted to relent, to give himself over to the longings ripping him apart, but he couldn't. He had a duty, an obligation to Greg, to God, to protect her. His honor wouldn't allow him to let this go on. He disengaged from her, setting her back on her pointed ballet shoes. "This is wrong. I can't take advantage of you."

She stared at him as if he'd slapped her. "Take advantage? Hello! I'm the one taking."

"What's this about?" he asked, his voice ragged to his own ears. "Your frenzied dancing, the kiss. This isn't you."

"It's the only way I can deal with the pain," she cried, whirling away from him. "When I'm dancing, the world goes away. When I kiss you…" She let loose a bitter, desperate laugh. "Though why I would want anything from you is beyond me." Her gaze hardened. "It's because of you that I lost my father long before he was murdered."

He drew back. Where was this coming from? "What are you talking about?"

She scoffed. Her fists clenched at her side. "I'm talking about all the time he spent with you. Time that should have been mine."

Feeling like he was lost in a foggy haze, Ben tried to make sense of what she was saying. "I don't understand. Your father loved you dearly and spent every moment he could with you."

"Hardly. You were the one he took fishing and camping. You were the one he invited to the Spurs games."

"Because you were here," Ben pointed out.

"You spent practically every waking moment dancing. What did you expect of your father?"

"To want to be with me," she stated in a sharp-edged voice.

"He did want to." Ben stared at her defiant, hurt expression in confusion. Did she really think her father had favored him over her? And still held that against him? "Corinna, your father wanted you to have everything you wanted. He wanted you to pursue your dream."

"But it wasn't my dream. It was my mother's!" she cried. Then her eyes widened with horror and she slapped a hand over her mouth. "I didn't mean that."

Stunned by her revelation, he reached out a hand to her. "Corinna—"

She let out a tortured groan, whirled around and ran out of the studio. Ben ran after her, but pulled up short when she entered the women's locker room.

Wiping a hand over his face, he leaned against the wall to wait. He hadn't realized she resented him, nor had he realized how she felt about her dancing. He could only imagine how she must be feeling right now. He'd never been in a situation like this, always preferring to keep people at an emotional distance, but with Corinna he couldn't seem to do that.

He'd made a mess of things. He didn't know how to reach out to her, to heal her. Wasn't sure he really wanted to. But he had to. He'd made a promise.

Deep in his spirit he felt a groaning sigh working its way up.

"Oh, Lord, please," he whispered. "I don't know what to do."

For I will turn their mourning to joy.

The words from the Bible in the book of Jeremiah came to him, offering him comfort. Not by his power but by God's. He clung to that promise. If only Corinna would be open to God's healing.

Somehow, someway, God would show him how to help her.

A high-pitched scream, abruptly cut off, shattered the quiet. Ben's heart pitched. Fear revved his blood.

In a frantic motion, he pushed away from the wall and banged into the locker room. A man wearing a black ski mask had Corinna by the throat, his big, beefy hands squeezing her tender flesh. She fought, clawing at his arms, kicking with her feet.

How had he entered the building? Ben's hand

went to his holstered gun. But he knew getting off a clean shot in such tight quarters would be tricky. The assailant only had to whip Corinna around and she'd be in his line of fire.

Corinna's panicked eyes sought his before they rolled back.

White-hot lightning rage flashed through Ben, propelling him over the wooden bench. He slammed into the assailant, sending him crashing sideways into the metal lockers and breaking his grip on Corinna.

She slid to the floor in an unconscious heap, distracting Ben for the split second it took for the man to come at Ben swinging, connecting with Ben's nose. He felt pain explode in his face. Tears immediately blinded him. Still, he lashed out, his fist glancing off the guy's cheekbone and another punch driving deep into his gut.

Another jabbing blow from the attacker to Ben's already broken nose drove Ben back to his knees. Bright lights blurred his vision. He tried to grab the attacker by the waist, but the assailant twisted away, eluding Ben's grasp.

The sound of running footsteps echoed inside the tiled locker room. Then the assailant was gone.

When his vision cleared, Ben scrambled to

Corinna's side. His face throbbed. No matter how many times he'd experienced a broken nose, the pain was still the worst. But he knew it would eventually die away. Checking Corinna's pulse, he assured himself she was breathing before pulling out his cell phone to call 911 and then his team.

As he waited for help to arrive, he smoothed back a lock of hair that had come loose from her bun, leaving a trail of his blood smeared across her cheek. He yanked his hand back, hating that he'd marred her perfection. Hated even more the dark bruises showing up on the translucent skin of her neck where her attacker had tried to choke her.

The guy's build matched Corinna's description of the man who'd broken into her home. Possibly the same man who'd murdered Greg. Impotent fury tightened Ben's gut. He'd had the slimeball within his clutches and he'd let him get away.

He slammed a fist into the metal locker next to him.

"Ben? Is he gone?"

His breath caught at Corinna's soft voice, and he turned his attention to her. Tenderness constricted his chest. She blinked up at him with wide, trusting eyes. If anything had happened... He swallowed back the bile that rose.

At least he'd managed to save her life.

"Yes, he's gone. You're safe." He cupped her face. "Thank God you're all right."

"God didn't save me. You did."

He shook his head. "Make no mistake. God saved you. Because He loves you."

Her gaze shifted away. Clearly she didn't share his opinion. It hurt to think she didn't believe what he'd said. Whatever else Ben did, he was going to make sure she knew just how much God loved her.

The sound of the ambulance arriving halted additional conversation. Ben helped Corinna to her feet. Together they met the paramedics and the police. He wasn't surprised to see Daniel and Anderson arrive. He knew the rest of the Rangers were tied up on other cases.

After having his broken nose set and bandaged, Ben gave a description of the perp to the responding officers. Then he checked with the paramedics, who assured him Corinna's bruises would heal. There'd been no permanent damage to her throat, and her momentary loss of consciousness was due to lack of oxygen. Though she'd have a headache for a while, she'd be fine.

They released them both with the promise that they'd follow up with their respective doctors.

After briefing the two Rangers, Ben drove Corinna to Gisella's. The house was dark when they arrived. No one answered when he knocked. Corinna let them in with the spare key Gisella had given her. She'd changed her clothes before leaving the dance studio, and now wore a lightweight sweat suit that covered her from neck to ankle but still managed to make her look tiny and breakable and yet very feminine. She appealed to Ben on so many levels. Levels best unexplored.

Collecting his thoughts, he called Gisella's cell phone. She answered on the third ring. "Hernandez."

"It's Ben. We're at your house."

"Did you get my message?"

He sighed. In all the commotion, he hadn't thought to check. "No. What's up?"

"I'm at the office filling out the paperwork on the hostage situation. Perp was taken out. All hostages were recovered unharmed."

"Good." He told her what had transpired at the dance studio.

"You're both okay?" she asked, her voice heavy with concern.

"Yeah. I'll wait here with Corinna until you arrive."

"I'll be there as soon as I can," Gisella promised before hanging up.

"Looks like you're stuck with me for a while longer."

"I'm okay with that." Corinna met his gaze. A smoldering fire lit the dark depths of her eyes.

His pulse jumped. His gaze dropped to her mouth where she worried the velvety softness of her full bottom lip with her straight white teeth. The yearning to kiss her grabbed a hold of him.

She leaned against the back of the couch, as if she needed the piece of furniture to hold her up.

Forcing himself to push away the current of attraction pulling at him, he said, "Maybe you should go lie down."

Her lips twisted in a wry grimace. "I couldn't sleep right now if I wanted to. My nerves are shot. How did that guy get in?"

Aching with regret at all she'd suffered, he said, "He pried open the locker-room window. It won't happen again."

"Where's my gun? You never gave it back to me."

He frowned. "Locked up. I'll protect you."

She gave him a pointed look. "You can't be

everywhere at once. I need to be able to defend myself."

His gut clenched. "You could too easily be overpowered and the gun used against you. Or you could hurt someone and have to live with that for the rest of your life. Even when it's a bad guy, shooting someone takes a toll. Self-defense classes would better serve you."

She contemplated his words. Then nodded. "I'll look into some. I did take a class years ago. But a refresher course would be good." Her gaze landed on the bandage across his nose. "Does it hurt?"

He shrugged. "It's just a broken nose. I've had them before. It'll heal."

She cocked her head to the side. "You've had your nose broken more than once before? What happened?"

Uncomfortable with the direction of the conversation because he didn't want to probe old wounds, he said, "Are you hungry? I'm sure I can find something to make."

He headed into the kitchen. She followed, obviously not about to relent. "Was it on the job?"

"One time."

"How many more times?"

"A couple." He turned away to search the

cupboards. He laid out a bowl, a fry pan and a whisk.

Which would make this the fourth time he'd had his nose broken, she thought. That couldn't be good. Curiosity rose, prompting her to ask, "When did the other two times happen?"

He rummaged through the refrigerator, pulling out eggs, scallions and mushrooms. "When I was a kid."

"Did you fall or something?"

"No." He cracked eggs into a bowl and whipped them up.

"A fight, then?"

"Yeah, sort of." Keeping his gaze on his task, he began chopping the vegetables.

Corinna tapped her foot. Why the evasive answer? "Sort of? How can you sort of be in a fight?"

When he glanced up, his expression clearly stated he didn't want to delve into this. "Leave it alone."

She really should. She hadn't wanted to be drawn emotionally to him. She'd tried to set a boundary the day he'd come to the shelter and watched her teach. The way he'd been with sweet little Gretchen had melted her heart and made her realize she needed to stay far away from him.

She was beginning to see he was the type of man she could fall for. In a big way. The type of man who could break her heart. And she'd been right to think getting too close was a bad idea. Look how she'd behaved when he'd come to the studio. She'd practically thrown herself at him and he'd rejected her again.

But he'd saved her life and suffered an injury for her sake. That counted for a lot.

And she was curious about him. What had her father seen in Ben that made him take the teen under his wing all those years ago?

She didn't know much about his upbringing, only that he had no family, which was why her father had always invited him to share in their holidays. After her mother's death, her dad had been all she'd had. Being forced to share him with the interloper had chafed at her already wounded heart.

She'd stubbornly refused to take an interest in Ben. She felt bad about that now. But she couldn't undo her selfish, childish behavior. She could only move forward. "Who did you fight with?"

He dumped the eggs in the buttered, sizzling fry pan. "You really want to know?"

She nodded.

As he fluffed the eggs while slowly dropping

in the scallions and mushrooms and spices he'd found in the cupboard, he sighed. "The first time with another foster kid. He was three years older and mean. He didn't like that I said no when he wanted my food."

She hadn't known he'd grown up in foster care. Her dad had never told her. Compassion infused her, questions bombarded her mind. "How old were you?"

"Eight."

A deep ache squeezed her chest until she could barely breathe. Eight? Still just a baby. She couldn't imagine. "What happened to your parents?"

He took two plates from a cupboard and set them on the counter. "Both dead."

She put her hand to her mouth as tears welled. "I'm so sorry."

He divided up the eggs without so much as glancing at her. "Don't be. My father was a drug dealer, killed during a bad deal. My mother was a junkie. She ODed when I was five."

"While you were at school?" *Please let him say yes.*

"No. I found her when I got up one morning."

Her hand covered her heart. "Oh, no. That's horrible."

He shrugged. "Since I was already deemed at risk because of my mom's drug use, when I didn't come to school for three days, child protective services came knocking."

Sympathy gripped her, filling her with the desire to reach out to touch him, offer some sort of comfort. "I'm so sorry. That must have been devastating."

"I survived."

The matter-of-fact way he spoke ripped her up inside. He couldn't be that well-adjusted, could he?

He'd been so young. So alone.

She thought back to when her father had brought Ben around for the first time. At nineteen there'd been something dark and dangerous about him. Now she understood. He was an orphan, raised in a system that didn't always work. That left scars.

"How can you speak of this without any emotion?"

He cocked his head. "What should I feel? Sorry for myself?"

She couldn't imagine this man feeling self-pity. He was too self assured, too pragmatic. But she'd expect sorrow at the very least. "Do you remember your parents?"

He gave a slow nod. A flash of sadness darkened his eyes. He wasn't as unfeeling as he wanted her to believe. "I do. I have a few clear memories, some good. Some bad."

"I hope I never lose my memories," she stated, aching for him and for herself. She had no problem indulging in a bout of self-pity. She struggled to keep from sliding down that road.

Ben came around the counter and took her hand. "You won't. I'll help you to remember."

She squeezed his hand. "I'll hold you to that."

A noise at the front door raised the hair at the back of her neck. "It's Gisella."

Ben tugged her off the stool and around the counter, positioning himself in front of her. "We can't be sure." He unholstered his weapon, his hand covering the grip, his finger hovering over the trigger.

Corinna latched on to Ben's arm. His muscles tensed beneath her fingers.

The front door swung open. Gisella walked in and drew up short when she saw them. "Whoa. You didn't tell me you had a busted nose."

With relief, Corinna stepped out from behind Ben and proudly said, "He saved my life."

Red crept up Ben's neck. "Just doing my job."

He picked up a plate and handed it to Corinna. "You got here quick. Just in time for some food."

"No traffic." Gisella, looking a bit stunned, moved into the kitchen. Her gaze rested on Corinna. "Was it the same guy from the house?"

Corinna nodded and set the plate of steaming eggs on the counter in front of Gisella. "We think so."

"He in custody?"

Ben shook his head. "Nope. Got away."

Catching this guy was personal on many levels for Ben. Corinna could only imagine the disappointment running through him. She touched his arm. "You'll get him."

He met her gaze. Guilt brightened his hazel eyes. "I should have shot him when I had the chance."

Cocking her head, she asked, "Why didn't you?"

Gentleness softened his expression. "I didn't want to risk hitting you."

She was touched and a little disconcerted that he had put her welfare over capturing a criminal. Had his feelings for her grown deeper than just wanting to do his job? "Well, I thank you."

Their gazes held. For a moment, she thought

she saw affection in his eyes. She was still trying to sort out what she felt. Gratitude for sure. That was easy to admit to.

"This smells delicious," Gisella interjected. "Thanks. To…?" Her questioning gaze danced between Ben and Corinna.

Corinna gestured with her fork at Ben. "Him."

Gisella looked impressed. "Who knew you could cook."

Ben frowned. "It's just eggs."

Gisella set her Stetson to the side. "You'd be surprised how many guys don't even know how to make simple scrambled eggs without burning them. Or wouldn't think to add veggies." She dug her fork into the fluffy concoction. "Mmm."

Corinna took a few bites. The eggs tasted good, but her stomach churned as soon as the food hit bottom. She set her fork down to drink some water.

"You're not eating," Ben admonished.

"My tummy's upset," she said.

Ben and Gisella exchanged a look that Corinna couldn't quite name. "What was that?"

Ben raised his eyebrows. "What was what?"

This was worse than being in the principal's office in grade school. Her father and Principal

Kaplan had exchanged looks that spoke of private conversations revolving around her. That same sort of look had just passed between Ben and Gisella. Wagging her index finger between the two, she said, "That look."

Gisella grimaced.

Ben met her gaze directly. "We're concerned. You haven't been eating or sleeping well. You've been pushing yourself too hard."

She felt slightly betrayed because he couldn't know any of that unless Gisella was reporting to him. It didn't matter he was Gisella's boss while on the job. Corinna just hadn't realized living here would be part of Gisella's job time. How irritating to know her life was so scrutinized.

"I'm a big girl." What made him think he had some say in her life, anyway? "I can take care of myself. I know my limits and my limitations. I don't need either one of you mothering me."

Ben held up his hands, palms out. "Whoa. Calm down."

Insulted by his condescending tone, Corinna straightened to her full five feet four inches. "I *am* calm."

Gisella rose, care and concern on her face plain to read. "Corinna, we're not trying to mother you. We care about you."

"Because you have to," Corinna muttered, wondering if they'd be so considerate if she weren't Captain Pike's daughter. She knew Ben wouldn't. He'd already confessed his attention was the byproduct of a promise. Who knew he'd end up being such an honorable guy? Or that she'd find herself wishing he'd see her as more than just an obligation. A duty. A debt repaid.

Suddenly very tired and overwrought, she said, "I'm going to say good night now."

"I'm here if you need anything," Gisella said, her gaze echoing the sincerity in her voice.

Deciding that Gisella's concern was genuine, Corinna smiled her thanks.

Ben came to her side and gathered her hands in his. Warmth traveled up her arms and spread throughout her body.

"I'm not going to let that guy get anywhere near you again. I promise."

The heartfelt determination in his tone touched Corinna. Was he being driven by more than just his duty or need to repay a debt? He seemed to be taking her safety personally, as if she really mattered on a heart level.

And did she care if his attention was something deeper? She honestly didn't know, and really wasn't in any frame of mind to examine her feelings too closely.

Confused, she tugged her hands free and backed away with a quick good-night. She hoped in the light of day her feelings would become clear. One way or another.

TEN

The next morning, Ben arrived at Gisella's house just as the female Ranger and Corinna were getting into Gisella's vehicle. His heart gave a little jolt at the sight of Corinna, so young and fresh. The epitome of goodness and light.

Shaking off the strange effect she had on him, Ben climbed from his Jeep and started walking toward the ladies. The quiet September morning was heavy with humidity. Overhead birds flew in a V formation across a blue sky.

Gisella leaned on the open door of her car while Corinna walked toward him as he came up the drive. His gaze roamed over her, appreciating the view.

In deference to the day's coming heat, the pale yellow summer dress Corinna had chosen to wear showed her curves to advantage, reminding him how those curves felt pressed against him. Her dark hair was up in its customary bun at the nape of her slender neck.

Sometimes he wished she'd let her hair fall loose about her shoulders. His fingers itched to feel the silky softness. Her dark eyes regarded him with curiosity and something else he couldn't quite identify, making him curious as to what she really thought of him.

He didn't see the familiar coldness or the haughtiness that had always made him feel that she found him lacking.

"Good morning." She halted in front of him, blocking the way. "Why are you here?"

He touched the brim of his Stetson. "Morning. I thought I'd take you to breakfast before you hit the studio."

Mild surprise crinkled the corners of her mouth.

"That is, if you haven't already eaten," he added, though he'd be surprised if she said yes.

She shook her head. "No, I haven't eaten."

Confirming his suspicion.

For a split second she seemed to contemplate his plan. "Where would you like to go?"

Pleasantly surprised, he said, "I know this great little café on the Riverwalk that makes the best French crepes this side of the Atlantic."

Cleary intrigued, she said, "Really? How did you know I love crepes?"

A twinge of sadness made his smile falter. "Your father."

"He told you?" Tears welled in her eyes.

He nodded. "He made them every Sunday after church, right?"

With a soft sigh, she said, "Right."

"Today's not Sunday, but I thought…"

"That would be nice," Corinna said.

Gisella cleared her throat, drawing their attention. "What's the plan, guys?"

Ben glanced over at her. "She's coming with me."

Gisella's knowing smile made heat crawl up his neck. Why was he feeling embarrassed? He was just doing his job. Taking Corinna to breakfast fell under the header of protection. Shoving his discomfort away, he took Corinna's dance bag and led her to his Jeep.

Twenty minutes later they arrived at the café on the Riverwalk. An interesting establishment with dark wood paneling and large glossy photos of France decorating the walls.

"We'll sit inside," Ben told the hostess who greeted them at the reception desk.

"No, we won't. We'll sit outside," Corinna countered. She wanted to enjoy the early morning sunshine.

"You'd be too exposed out there," Ben said, his gaze rife with meaning.

The last thing she wanted was him hovering over her like some snarling beast, hyperaware of any perceived threat. That was no way to live. "I'm not living my life in fear. I'll take my chances." She walked past him, out to the patio seating area, forcing him to follow.

Taking the table by the edge of the shale-floored space, she sat and enjoyed the view. The colorful table umbrella provided shade from the morning sun. Sunlight, filtered through the lush greenery and full trees along the walking path located parallel to the river, dappled the water.

If it were later in the day, crowded flat-bottom boats would float past, their occupants avidly enthralled by cruise narrators as they relayed the history of the Riverwalk.

Ben sat down opposite her. "I don't like this. You take too many chances with your safety."

"I don't mean to make your job harder, but I meant what I said. I'm not going to cower in a corner. My father wouldn't have. And neither would you."

"But that's different."

She arched an eyebrow. "Because I'm a woman?"

He pressed his lips together and didn't answer. Smart man.

They ordered and soon their meal was before them. The soothing setting made the tension in Corinna's shoulders lessen as she sat back and sipped orange juice from a tall glass. She'd finished her crepe with gusto. Ben had been right, this café made a great crepe. She could get used to spending time with Ben like this, enjoying his company. Though she would have liked for him to relax a bit. His attentive gaze took everything in, looking for some threat.

"This is nice," she said, content to just sit and unwind. "Thank you for thinking of it."

Ben's big, strong hands wrapped around his coffee mug. "You're welcome. I know these past few days have been difficult."

She looked away toward the arched stone bridge spanning the river. Her mood crashed down, dispelling the contentment of moments before. "Difficult."

Would she ever be able to move on? Would Ben? She ached to think they would always have this bond of grief between them. Regret for losing the short-lived sense of happiness and peace cascaded through her. She sighed. "Yeah, difficult is an understatement."

Ben reached across the table to cover one of her hands. His strong fingers wrapped around hers—the contact at once pleasing yet painful. He was her last connection to her dad.

So much had happened the past few days. Her view of Ben had shifted. She was finding it harder with each passing moment to hold on to the old resentment and anger. Compassion and affection were rapidly healing the wounds of her youth.

And now she wasn't sure what to think or how to deal with her changing feelings for Ben. She'd always had strong feelings for him, these were just different. She liked him, really liked him. But what did that mean for the future? Did she want it to mean anything?

She honestly didn't know.

"What did you mean when you said dancing wasn't your dream, but your mother's?" Ben asked.

She nearly groaned. She'd hoped he'd forgotten she'd let her secret slip. How could she explain? "I didn't mean to say that."

"Is it true, though? If dancing wasn't your

dream then why have you devoted your life to it and worked so hard at it?"

Raw emotions scraped at her nerves. Grief, guilt, a touch of anger all neatly forged together to make a sharp knife of regret. "You know that my mother was once a prima ballerina, right?"

"Yes, Greg told me."

"She danced all over the country, until she came here to San Antonio and met my father. She left the stage to raise me." Corinna bit her bottom lip. "I wasn't exactly the daughter she'd hoped for."

Ben's eyebrows drew together. "How can that be true? She'd be proud of you."

Corinna gave a small humorless laugh. "You don't understand. From the very first I was a tomboy. I wanted to be like my father."

Clearly surprised, Ben stared at her. "You're kidding. I had no idea."

She shrugged. "Why would you?" She shook her head, thinking back to those early days of childhood. "I was such a terror. Mom tried so hard to turn me into a little ballerina. Dance classes galore, recitals and girly dresses. All I wanted was to be like my dad. I didn't understand why I couldn't wear a badge and fake holster with a pop gun to dance class."

That made Ben smile. "I can see it now." He held up his hand like he were reading a marquee. "Corinna, the Dancing Ranger."

She held his gaze and managed a small laugh through the tightness constricting her throat. Dishes crashed nearby. A clumsy waiter clearing a table. Ben tensed as his gaze sought any possible danger. He returned his gaze to her.

The humor died away. Tension knotted her shoulders. "But then she got sick. Breast cancer. Stage four by the time it was discovered."

Sympathy etched lines in his handsome face.

She dropped her gaze to the table as the memories haunted her. Ben's gentle squeeze to her hand gave her the impetus to go on. Taking a bracing breath, she said, "I didn't understand at first why she was so tired all the time. Why she kept going to the doctors. Why she and Dad seemed so sad. Why she cried so often. I got scared, started acting out—getting into fights, talking back to the teachers at school."

Shame built in her chest. "I was eleven and no one was talking to me. Finally, Dad lost his temper and yelled at me to stop making things so hard for my mother. *Why couldn't I just behave and do as she asked?*" She met Ben's compassionate gaze. "That was the only time I ever saw him lose his temper."

"I'm sure he was hurting."

She nodded. "Not long after that my mom told me she was dying." Tears sprang to the surface. She fought them back. "I still remember the smell of her perfume, the feel of her petal-soft skin as she held me while I cried. I begged and pleaded with her not to die." A horrible sound escaped her closing throat. "Like she had a choice."

"I'm sure she understood. You were young."

"Young and selfish."

"Corinna—"

"Don't." She couldn't tolerate platitudes. "You asked me why I dance. It's because her last words to me were 'Dance for me, baby. Be my ballerina.'"

He nodded in understanding. "So that's what you did."

She wiped at a stray tear and blinked several times. "Yes. That's what I did. Dancing became my refuge. When I dance nothing else exists." She gave a self-effacing laugh. "But I still wanted to be like my father."

Ben leaned forward, his expression earnest. "And you are. You have all of his good qualities."

A teasing light entered his hazel eyes. "And a few of his not so good."

Arching an eyebrow, she said, "Not so good?"

"Stubborn, focused, perfectionist." The corner of his mouth tipped up in a teasing grin. "Ring any bells?"

She made a face at him. "I think I'd rather hear about the good qualities."

His eyes twinkled. "Give me a second to come up with those."

"Hey!" She looked at him through her lowered lashes. He was something special, this man who made her laugh, who made her want to move forward with her life.

He sobered. "Seriously, you are a lot like your father. Kind, generous, loyal."

Her cheeks flamed at the complimentary words. "So are you." She kept her tone light to regain the peace and serenity that had started off the day.

He tilted his head. "Is that a good thing or not?"

"It's good." She surprised herself at how true those words were and even more surprised by the pride she felt for Ben. He'd come from such a hard beginning and had become a man worth admiring. She admired him in a way she'd never felt before. And that was very appealing.

"Your approval means a lot." His expression turned pensive. "I'm sorry you felt left out of your father's life. If I had known…" he trailed off.

She waved away his needless guilt. "I doubt your knowing would have changed my behavior."

"Maybe not. But maybe I would have tried to draw you out more. Or at least tried to understand."

"All water under the bridge now."

"Having your father take an interest in me saved my life."

Curiosity made her want to know more. "How so?"

"I was headed down a destructive road that would have ended badly. I owe your father so much."

The reminder of why he was taking such a personal interest in her tasted bittersweet. He owed her father. She was just a job even if at times it seemed like so much more.

Resigned to the boundaries of their relationship, she said, "It's getting late. I need to head to the studio. We've only a couple more days of rehearsal left until the charity fund-raiser."

Ben stood and laid several bills on the table. Corinna rose and tried to squelch the growing affection blossoming in her heart, but she had the feeling that would be like telling the sun to stop shining.

She put her hand into his outstretched one and stepped forward just as a loud crack of a gun split the air. Corinna felt a puff of hot air pass by her as the bullet barely missed her head.

Birds squawked, people screamed as they hit the deck and Ben jerked her to the ground. Corinna's gaze swung toward the walkway, searching for the shooter.

Another shot rang out. Bits of shale from the patio floor burst near Corinna's leg. Sharp fragments stung her flesh.

"Come on," Ben barked. "We have to get out of here. Stay down!"

In a crouch, he led Corinna away from the restaurant toward the staircase that would take them to the street level. They crossed against traffic and ran to the parking garage.

Corinna threw a glance over her shoulder. There didn't seem to be anyone following them. Her heart pounded painfully in her chest as she slid into the passenger seat of Ben's Jeep.

Ben started the engine, threw the gear into drive and squealed out of the parking lot. With quick efficiency, he called the shooting in.

"That was too close," he said after hanging

up the phone. His knuckles turned white as he gripped the steering wheel.

Ben had saved her life again. Though she doubted he'd see it that way. He'd say God had had a hand in this. Well, if that were true, then God must be very proud of Ben, because he was a true hero.

If she weren't careful, she'd find herself falling in love with Ben. And that was a scary thought on so many levels.

Once Ben was driving through the downtown traffic, the rush of adrenaline abated. He'd phoned in the shooting, though figured the sniper was long gone. CSU would find the spent bullets. He hoped they matched the bullets that killed Greg. Then they'd know for sure if they were after the same man.

Feeling calmer, but still on the alert, Ben cracked the window to let in some air. The day was turning into a South Texas scorcher. The temperature gauge on the dashboard read just past eighty degrees and rising.

He stole a glance at Corinna. Though pale and obviously shaken, she was holding up beautifully.

He'd never had as much trouble keeping a

witness safe before. Corinna was certainly trouble with a capital T.

Hearing her story touched him deeply. She was more complicated and stronger than he'd ever imagined. And he found himself drawn to her with each passing moment. He admired that she hadn't panicked when the shots rang out. She was more like her father than she even knew.

Glancing in the rearview mirror as he wove through the morning commuters, he noticed a white four-door sedan trailing behind them. He couldn't make out the driver's face. Only the driver's mouth, set in a grim line, was visible beneath the car's sun visor and the driver's baseball cap. Could it be the shooter?

Just to be sure he wasn't letting paranoia get to him, Ben made a sharp right-hand turn on screeching tires down an alley.

"Hey!" Corinna clung to the hand hold over the passenger door.

"We're being followed," Ben said as the white sedan made the same turn.

Corinna whipped around to look out the back window. Ben slowed as they approached a busy intersection. He tried to judge the timing of the passing cars in hopes of crossing the traffic without getting slammed by oncoming traffic. He started to pull into the intersection.

The horn from a city bus blared from the left.

Ben hit the brakes. "Hang on!"

The white car smashed into the back end of the Jeep.

Corinna screamed.

The squeal of tires accelerating on pavement coming from the white vehicle sent a shudder through Ben as the sedan pushed the Jeep into the path of the oncoming bus. He braced himself for impact. The bus swerved, clipping the front end of the Jeep, sending them spinning into oncoming traffic. Ben's head bounced off the side window and pain exploded inside his head.

A big green SUV rammed into the rear passenger side, smoke billowing from the antilock brakes as the driver tried to stop his forward progress.

The strap of the seat belt dug across Ben's chest. The explosion of metal clashing with metal from surrounding cars colliding echoed in Ben's ears. The Jeep came to a vibrating halt.

Ben gave his head a shake to clear his vision and his rattled brain. Horror rushed in. Corinna!

She was slumped over with her eyes closed, the seat belt keeping her upright. Blood from a cut to her head bled. He quickly checked her pulse. Thready. He undid his seat belt and moved to ease her back against the seat. She moaned.

He breathed a sigh of relief that she was coming around.

"Thank you, Lord, for helping me keep her alive. I couldn't do this without You."

He looked out the smashed back window. The white sedan was gone.

The wail of a siren meant help was on the way.

"Hang on, Corinna," he said as he stroked back a loose lock of hair. A deep, tender aching welled in his chest, unfamiliar, yet somehow right. He wasn't sure what to make of his growing attachment to Corinna. And now was not the time to try to figure it out.

A police cruiser arrived on the scene and began directing traffic as more police drove up. Moments later an ambulance pulled to a stop and two paramedics jumped out.

He climbed out of the vehicle as the paramedics reached the Jeep. "I'm fine, but she's hurt."

The bus listed to the right. Bent metal and broken glass littered the road. The street looked like a destruction derby.

One of the paramedics went to the Jeep's

passenger side. The other stayed with Ben. "Sir, I think you should sit. You've a nasty bruise on your head."

Ben waved him away. He needed to talk with the police officer. "It's just a bump." Ben started forward but the paramedic grabbed him by the arm.

"Sir, you could have a concussion. Let me check you out."

"After I talk with the officer," Ben said and yanked his arm free. He rushed to one of the SAPD officers and identified himself. "Hey, I need you to put out a BOLO on a white, four-door sedan." He rattled off the make and model as the officer wrote on a notepad. Hopefully the "Be on the look out" order would help them track down the car. "I got a partial of the license." The officer wrote the numbers down as Ben said them.

"I'll get this to dispatch," the officer said, then narrowed his gaze. "Ranger Fritz, you don't look so good."

As the charge of adrenaline began to wane, Ben realized how badly his head throbbed. His nose wasn't doing so hot, either. The world tilted as a wave of dizziness washed through him. He needed to check on Corinna. "I'm okay," he muttered.

Pushing through his own discomfort, he made his way back to her. The paramedics had moved her to a gurney and were wheeling her toward the waiting ambulance.

Ben's heart squeezed tight with dread and self-recriminations. She'd been hurt badly enough to warrant a trip to the hospital. This was his fault.

As he reached her side, she held out a hand for him.

"I'm okay, just a little cut. But they won't listen," she said.

She didn't look okay. A bandage covered the gash on her head. "I'll come with you."

She squeezed his hand. The paramedics lifted the gurney into the empty bay, and Ben climbed in beside her and took her hand. Tenderness expanded in his chest. What would he do if anything happened to her? The mere thought sent his stomach plummeting. He kissed her knuckles. "I'm so sorry."

"This wasn't your fault. That maniac in the car did this."

"I should have been paying better attention. I shouldn't have turned down that alley. I shouldn't have let us sit outside for breakfast."

Her expression turned contrite. "Stop beating yourself up. I should have listened to you. Again."

"Yes, you should have," he agreed gently.

"But we're alive and safe. That's all that matters."

Taking in a deep breath to calm his nerves, he slowly let it out. "You're right." He kissed her knuckles.

A blush brightened her cheeks and a pleased smile spread across her face. The impulse to fold her into his arms and kiss her gripped him. He had to shift his focus away from her lovely face. The last thing she needed was him confusing the situation with attraction.

At the hospital, they were both checked out by the ER doctor. After he declared that neither had a concussion or suffered serious harm they were released. Since Ben's Jeep was out of commission, he called for Anderson to come pick them up and take them to the Ranger's headquarters. Ben kept an alert eye out for any threats as they made their trek across town.

Cade met them at the door. His usually calm demeanor had an edge of anticipation. "We got a hit on that partial license number. The sedan was reported stolen last night."

"Figures," Ben said as he ushered Corinna to

his office. "Check with SAPD, see if the BOLO has come up with anything."

"Sure thing," Cade said and veered off to make the calls.

Corinna took a seat facing the desk. Her hands shook. She clasped them together and stared at the decorated walls. Sadness welled in her eyes. "I should box up my father's things."

Hit with sorrow at the suggestion, Ben's gaze drifted over the framed certificates and photos of the Pike family. Having Greg's things around gave Ben a sense of peace. "There's no hurry."

Her gaze met his with concern. "But you must want to put up your own certificates and pictures. This is your office now. You need to move on."

"The few certificates I have are tucked away in a box. But I suppose I could get them out."

"Pictures?"

He shrugged. "No happy family portraits except the ones with you and your father, remember?"

She winced. "I'm sorry."

Waving away her sympathy, he said, "Please, don't be. With your father's help and God's grace, I've forgiven my parents their flaws."

Tilting her head with curiosity in her lovely dark eyes, she said, "You really do have a deep sense of faith, don't you?"

"I do."

A look of wonder crossed her face. "Just like my father."

Sadness replaced the wonder. "He'd wanted me to embrace faith the same way. I tried." She let out a bitter noise. "What little good that did."

They'd covered this ground. Ben didn't know how to make her understand God wasn't to blame for her loss. So instead this time he concentrated on the most important truth. "God is good. And He loves you. Take a chance on letting Him in. What do you have to lose?"

"I don't know if I have it in me to trust Him," she replied, her voice soft and so full of sorrow.

"You do. I know you do. He will never give up on you. Don't give up on Him."

She seemed to consider what he'd said for a moment. Then her expression closed, shutting down any more conversation. "I'd like to leave now."

Resigned to letting the subject drop, he shook his head. "I don't think you should do the benefit show."

"Excuse me?" She bolted from the chair. "I'm not going to let this guy win. He's already ruined my life by murdering my father. I'm not going to let him take my dancing, too. You can't ask that of me."

Ben was glad to hear her lay the blame for Greg's death so firmly where it belonged. A little forward progress was a good thing. The benefit show was a logistical nightmare, but so was every time they went out in public. He wasn't surprised she didn't want to back out of the charity event.

Though she certainly wasn't making his job easy. But she wouldn't be Corinna if she rolled over and played dead. No, she was a fighter. Much stronger than he'd ever imagined.

But the question was, was he strong enough to keep from falling in love with her?

ELEVEN

Daniel Riley appeared in the doorway of Ben's office. "SAPD found the car."

Hoping for more good news, Ben asked, "The driver?"

"Unfortunately, long gone. He abandoned the vehicle in the parking lot of a convenience store. CSU is taking possession of the car. If they find anything, they'll let us know."

Disappointed, Ben stood. "Call my cell. I'll be with Corinna."

Daniel's gaze jumped from him to Corinna and back. "Okay. I heard you're out a vehicle. You want to take my truck?"

Grateful for the offer, Ben shook his head. "No need. I'll take a department vehicle. Thanks."

Ben switched gears as he remembered the assignment he'd given Daniel. "How did the Alamo committee meeting go?"

"It went well. There are a few things we need to smooth out, but nothing we can't handle."

Ben clapped Daniel on the back. "I appreciate you taking the lead on this, Daniel."

He touched his fingers to the brim of his hat. "Aim to serve."

"I know, which is why I put the paperwork in for your promotion."

Daniel inclined his head. "To which I'm much obliged."

Obligation had nothing to do with one aspect of being upper management Ben really enjoyed. Hard work and dedication had earned Daniel Riley the promotion. "Let me know if anything develops."

"Sure thing." Daniel dipped his head to Corinna. "Miss Pike." Then he left the office.

Ben turned his attention to Corinna. Extending his arm, he said, "Shall we?"

"Thank you." She linked her arm through his. "For everything."

"Don't thank me yet. Until we catch this guy, I'm your shadow."

"Glad to hear that."

He sucked in a breath at the look of obvious approval and something else in her eyes…something close to affection.

For a moment he had the same sinking feeling he'd had once, as a kid on a camping trip with one of his foster families, when he'd found himself trapped in a quicksand pit along the Rio Grande River. It had taken three people to drag him out.

Trouble was, he wasn't sure he wanted to be dragged out of this particular quicksand.

Corinna couldn't concentrate. She kept missing the steps.

"Cory, you okay?" Kyle asked for at least the fourth time.

She sighed. "Sorry. Where were we?"

"Let's start at the setup for the lift." Kyle went over to the iPod to reset the track.

Corinna moved to her position. She stared at Ben's reflection in the mirror. He leaned against the wall, his arms crossed over his chest, a scowl on his handsome face as he watched her and her dance partner move together around the hardwood floor.

For the past two days, he'd been true to his word. He'd shadowed her every move, sticking close except at night when he left her in Gisella's care. Come morning, she'd find him sitting in his car outside of Gisella's house. She suspected he'd gone home only long enough to change clothes.

Good thing her cat was used to being alone. The feline had made herself quite comfortable at Ben's. As comfortable as Corinna was becoming in his shadow. His attentive need to stand guard made her feel protected and safe, yes, but also cherished and special.

"Cory?"

She pulled her thoughts back to the dance. She'd missed her cue. "Sorry. Why don't we take a break?"

Kyle strode across the floor, moving with primal grace. Taller than her, he exuded the athletic abilities in his hard sculpted muscles indicative of male dancers. He stopped beside her, his green eyes concerned. "Is he bothering you? Should I make him leave?"

She followed his glance toward Ben. He definitely was bothering her, but not in the way Kyle thought. She'd never before felt self-conscious while dancing. Ben's presence made her jittery on so many levels.

The Texas Ranger straightened, his hands falling to his sides as if they'd jerked his chain. He looked ready to brawl. Obviously, he took his duty as her protector to the extreme. He reminded her of a pit bull—fighting was in their genes. Protecting was just a part of who Ben was. And she found she didn't mind.

Returning her attention to Kyle, she said, "I just need a few minutes."

Kyle's gaze darted between the two. "Okay. If you say so."

Corinna moved to the side and picked up a towel to wipe the sweat from her brow and neck.

Her guard dog stepped over. "You done?"

"Just a break." She studied his face. "You don't have to watch, you know."

He raised an eyebrow. "I want to make sure you're safe."

She swept a hand outward toward the room. "It's a closed space. No windows, one entrance. I think it'd be safe if you wanted to wait out in the hall."

Hazel eyes narrowed. "What, I make you nervous?"

Oh, on so many levels. "Actually, yes."

He looked taken aback at her answer. "I was joking. Am I really making you nervous?"

How could he not know his effect on her? "Yes. For two days you've been standing over there scowling like you want to hit something. I appreciate that you feel responsible for me and all, but really, if you don't want to be here that badly, assign someone else."

"It's not that I don't want to be here," he said. He shot a glance to Kyle, who sat stretching on the floor near the mirrored wall. "I just don't trust that guy. He checked out fine but…"

"What?" She let out a surprised laugh. "You checked him out? You can't possibly think Kyle has anything to do with the man who attacked me or killed my father. He's been my dance partner for two years."

Ben's expression turned inscrutable.

Corinna tried to make sense of things. He'd suspected Kyle of wrongdoing? The absurdity of the suggestion rocked her back a step. A thought crossed her mind, startling her and sending her heart into triple time. Could Ben be jealous of Kyle?

Talk about absurd. Yet…

Ben could only feel jealous if he felt something more than duty and obligation towards her. Right?

A pleased warmth spread through her.

But she clamped down on that tide.

She wasn't ready to examine her own feelings for Ben too closely. Not with her father's killer still on the loose and the threat to her life hanging over their heads. Still, she couldn't just let Ben twist in the wind.

She laid a hand on his chest, felt his heart thundering beneath her palm. "Kyle's engaged. His fiancée and I are good friends."

Tension visibly melted from his body. Ben's expression turned almost sheepish as he covered her hand with his and curled his fingers around hers. "I, uh—should check in. See if Cade has any news from CSU on the car."

"You probably should," she replied, keeping her voice as even as possible so he wouldn't hear the amusement dancing inside her, making her feel lighter than she had in the past few weeks.

She just hoped she didn't get carried away.

Ben sank onto a wicker chair in the waiting area outside the dance room. Wow, he'd just made a fool of himself.

He'd been jealous and she'd called him on it with a graciousness he admired. He had no right to be jealous. But he couldn't deny knowing Kyle was engaged put his mind at ease.

At ease? What was that about? As if Ben had staked a claim on Corinna. His mind reeled.

Taking off his Stetson and setting it beside him on the bench, he raked a hand through his hair.

He had it bad. He knew Kyle wasn't a physical threat to Corinna's safety. He'd done a thorough background check on him the day after Greg's murder.

No, the threat was only in Ben's head. *Jealous.* He didn't do jealous. At least he hadn't until now. But when he heard Kyle call her by a nickname, he couldn't hold back his wish that he was close enough to Corinna to give her a nickname.

What did that mean?

"Lord, forgive me," he whispered. He didn't want to be full of jealousy. The toxic emotion had no place in his life.

He'd dated over the years occasionally. Had even had two long-term, romantic relationships. But he'd never experienced any sort of jealousy while dating Simone or Tara. Both relationships had run their course and ended amicably.

Though in retrospect, Ben acknowledged his heart had never really been involved with either woman. He'd liked them, cared for them even, but not love. Never love.

He wished Greg were here to give him advice. He'd know what to tell Ben, would be able to help him navigate this foreign territory. Though Ben doubted Greg would be too appreciative to discover Ben loved his daughter.

That last thought blasted through him with the thrust of a missile launch, making him a bit lightheaded.

He loved Corinna.

Greg's daughter.

Shock like a wave of icy water filled his veins. Oh, man, this was bad. He had no business falling in love with Corinna and all the reasons why marched across his brain. She was off-limits. He was supposed to be protecting her. He wasn't good enough for her.

But the biggest reason of all came tearing to the forefront. He was afraid. Afraid to commit his heart for fear she'd leave, just as everyone else whom he'd loved had done.

Resolved to ignore the ache in his chest, he swiped his hat off the bench and headed inside the studio to watch Corinna dance. His only duty was to protect her. And nothing more.

Awareness zipped along Corinna's nerve endings before she even glanced in the mirror and her gaze collided with Ben's. The scowl was gone as he took a seat on a stack of mats at the back of the room.

She smiled. He returned the favor. Her heart hitched and she careened out of control on her pirouette. She quickly recovered and focused on her dance.

An hour later, Madame Martin, an elegant woman who once had been the prima ballerina for the Joffrey Ballet, glided into the room, followed by the full company. She clapped sharply, signaling the end of Corinna and Kyle's rehearsal time. Her sharp eyes missed nothing as she assessed the dancers.

"For tomorrow's event I expect you all to arrive prepared and on time for dress rehearsal," Madame intoned. The ballet troupe's director slid a glance toward Ben and then back to Corinna. "I have been assured all necessary precautions have been taken to keep everyone safe."

Corinna appreciated Madame's concern. She'd been upset and highly indignant to hear of the attempts on Corinna's life, especially the one here in the dance company's building. She ran a tight ship.

"Let's run through the whole program and then we'll call it a day," Madame said.

The full run-through went well. Anticipation bubbled in Corinna's blood. She couldn't wait to leap across the open-air stage of the Arneson River Theatre tomorrow. Only a smidge of apprehension slithered over her flesh, raising goose bumps as she used a towel to wipe away the sheen of perspiration glistening on her skin.

She gathered her things, hitched her dance bag over her shoulder and joined Ben at the door. He immediately reached for the bag. Liking his gentlemanly manners, she allowed him to carry the tote to the borrowed vehicle. His attention made her feel special. But she had to remind herself he was only doing his job. They weren't dating or anything. Still, nervous tension bounced around her stomach.

She sought a safe subject as he drove and since she was curious about his life outside of the Rangers, she asked, "What do you do for fun?"

Ben seemed surprised by her question. "Fish occasionally. Ride my dirt bike."

"Dad talked about me learning to ride, but we never got around to it," she said with a dose of sadness and regret.

There were so many things they'd talked about doing, but never had the chance. She used to blame her father's relationship with Ben as the reason they never followed through on their plans. But now she understood that her dancing had been the biggest obstacle to having father/daughter time.

Letting go of all that resentment and anger left her feeling a bit hollow.

"I'll teach you," Ben offered.

Her heart rate picked up. "To ride? Really? That would be awesome."

"How about next Saturday?"

She didn't have to even think about it. "Yes. Saturday."

He gave her a slight bemused lopsided grin. "It's a date, then."

A date? The word rippled through her, the ramifications at once scary and yet, so right.

A date. She held the promise of the word in her heart. She had no idea where a date would lead. But for the first time since she'd met Ben, she really wanted to explore a relationship with him.

And that left her feeling off-kilter and scared.

Ben's cell phone rang, jerking his attention away from the shocking fact that he'd just made a date with Corinna. Wow. Not the way he'd expected the conversation to go. The words had just popped out before he'd been able to filter them. Not smart. He'd have to be more careful. He answered his phone. "Fritz."

"Hey, CSU found a partial print on the car,"

Anderson said. "We got a match on one—Eddie Jimenez. A resident of Boot Hill, Texas, with a long record of misdemeanors in Cameron County."

"Why didn't his picture show up in the NCIC database?"

"From the sounds of it, they do things old school over in Cameron. The sheriff said we were lucky to have electronic access to their fingerprints since they'd just this past summer gained the capability to upload the files to the AFIS."

"Welcome to the twenty-first century," Ben remarked. "Get a BOLO out on Jimenez."

"Already done," Anderson replied.

Of course it was. Ben could count on his team. "Keep me informed."

"Will do." Anderson hung up.

Ben returned his phone to the breast pocket of his dress shirt and his attention back to weaving through traffic.

Excited energy radiated from Corinna. "They found him?"

"Not yet. But we have a name. Eddie Jimenez. Ring any bells?"

She shook her head. "How is he connected to my father?"

"Don't know. But I intend to find out."

* * *

The next day when Ben picked her up at Gisella's to take her to the Arneson River Theatre, she'd asked him to stop by the shelter on the way. He waited outside because of the no-men-inside rule.

"You'll get to watch the performance on video." Corinna stood with her back to the cold fireplace while the occupants of the shelter gathered in the living room around her. The worn furniture needed replacing and the carpet could use a shampoo. Corinna would make sure some of the proceeds from the benefit went to sprucing them up, as well as the kitchen remodeling and five new beds already planned.

"But it won't be the same," whined twelve-year-old Claire. Tall for her age and gangly with long dark hair, the young girl chafed at being cooped up in the shelter. Corinna sympathized with the girl, knowing how limiting the shelter was. But the safety of the women and children depended on those limits.

Corinna exchanged a sympathetic glance with the girl's mother, Pat. She had taken her daughter and five-year-old son out of a highly volatile situation where her husband's drinking had careened out of control.

"Honey, it's not safe," Pat stated quietly, resting a hand on her son's shoulder. His arm still sported a cast from her husband's alcohol-induced temper.

"Is it safe for us?" Gretchen asked her mother, Carol.

"Not yet, dear." Carol smoothed her daughter's curls from her face.

Anguish that these women and children suffered tore through Corinna. From the day she'd found out about the shelter five years ago, she'd wanted to do something to help. Volunteering her time to teach had been rewarding, but with money so tight in this economy, Corinna and some of the other volunteers brainstormed other ways to help. The idea for the benefit had been born.

Corinna had pleaded her case with the dance company and had been gratified when every dancer had said they would participate voluntarily. Through her father's connections with the city, they'd secured the theatre for the show. Other volunteers had worked tirelessly to promote the event and make it the social occasion for all of San Antonio.

But it meant that the recipients of the proceeds couldn't come out of hiding since the shelter's name was on everything. Some of these women had husbands or boyfriends who were searching for them. Annie Nelson had been adamant that the location of the shelter remain a secure oasis for those who sought help. Corinna wished she could do more.

"Why don't we send Miss Corinna off with a prayer?" Annie asked as she came to stand beside Corinna.

Uncomfortable with the idea, Corinna tried not to grimace. She still felt at odds with God. She wasn't really sure she could trust in Him. But she sure wouldn't do anything to convey her negative feelings in front of the children.

She knew for many of the refugees seeking solace at the shelter, having faith in a loving God who was bigger and better than anything on earth, was sometimes the only sense of hope they had.

Just because her own faith had faltered didn't mean she had the right to make others stumble.

Several children raised their hands, eager to be called on to say the prayer as was tradition in the shelter. Annie winked at Corinna and then pointed to a little red-haired boy with a smattering of freckles across the bridge of his nose. "Joshua, would you like to say the prayer?"

The boy's face lit up. "Yes, ma'am." He bowed his head.

For a moment Corinna hesitated. She hadn't prayed since before her father's death. She wasn't ready to talk to God. Her gaze collided with Gretchen's big blue, curious eyes. A softening spread over Corinna's heart. Just enough that she could bow her head and close her eyes.

"Dear Father God, please be with Miss Corinna and the other dancers tonight. Don't let anyone fall and get hurt. Let the people pay lots of money so we can get a new kitchen. Amen."

Corinna pressed her lips tight to keep from chuckling at the innocent request for funds as she murmured "Amen." She opened her eyes and smiled at Joshua. "Thank you, kind sir."

Pleased with himself, the boy grinned back. His mother, a thin woman who still showed signs of abuse in the black and blue marring the skin around her left eye mouthed *Thank you* to Corinna. Aching for her, Corinna acknowledged the woman's gratitude with a slight nod.

Annie put her arm around Corinna's shoulders. "Let me walk you out." At the door, Annie said, "You tell your fella he best keep you safe tonight."

"Do you mean Captain Fritz?"

"I do mean that tall, handsome specimen of male beauty who came to check up on you. I wasn't so sure of him at first, but…" She tsked. "That man has it bad for you. He saved your life and was so sweet to the kids. He's a keeper."

Corinna could feel her cheeks heat up. "It's not like that."

Annie's shrewd gaze pinned Corinna in place. "Honey, I saw the way you were looking at that cowboy when he was charming little Gretchen. There's no way I'm believing you aren't sweet on him, too."

Well, that was unexpected and disconcerting. Corinna hadn't realized her feelings had been so transparent. But more important, could what she said about Ben be true?

A spurt of hope blossomed in her chest, making her heart rate pick up. She couldn't wait to find out.

The open-air venue of the Arneson River Theatre situated on the south side of the San Antonio River made for a security nightmare. The balmy evening only added to making Ben's nerves stretch so taut he was sure they'd snap at any second.

SAPD and the Rangers were patrolling the

vicinity, each having memorized Jimenez's face. Ben surveyed the structure from his vantage point behind a tall free-standing floodlight set in a recessed spot off to the right of the stage. At the moment only half the lights were turned on.

There were no wings on stage to speak of. Behind the stage, serving as the only backdrop, was a tall brick wall with three mission-style bell tower arches. A theater house with a red-tile roof sat adjacent to the stage which served the purposes of a backstage. With the added draw of tonight's benefit performance, the grassy-sloped seating area for 800 facing the stage overflowed with attendees. The river separated the audience from the stage, allowing the tour cruise boats to pass by.

Ben wasn't as concerned about the multitude of paying audience members—every person had been scanned with a wand and their belongings searched—as he was about the walking paths and the canal. There was no way to control who wandered by on the concrete trail that wound behind the stage or who had access to the stone footbridge connecting the two sides of the river. The mayor had refused his request to restrict access to the trails or to stop the flat-bottom boat tours from cruising down the river past the edge of the stage.

Frustrated with the limits to their security measures, Ben had stationed officers at both the entrance and exit points for the cruise boats, along the winding paths, on the rooftops of the restaurants and strategically around the theatre. They were as ready as they could be. Hopefully, Jimenez would show himself. And not hole up with a high-powered scope rifle. Ben's blood ran cold.

The dancers waited inside the theatre building to the left of the stage. Gisella was there with Corinna. She was safe for now. He had a direct line of sight to the door where the dancers would emerge as he waited for the show to begin.

A female local news anchor stepped to center stage with a handheld microphone. "Ladies and gentlemen, I'm Addison Reese, your host this evening. Welcome and thank you for attending tonight's benefit show for Miriam's Shelter. I'd like to introduce you to a very special lady who can tell you about this amazing shelter. Please welcome one of San Antonio's own, Prima Ballerina Miss Corinna Pike."

Ben stiffened. She hadn't mentioned she'd be addressing the audience. "Everyone stay alert,"

Ben ground out into the mic attached to his collar.

The hairs on his nape rose. His heart rate sped up. Standing still on stage would make her easy pickings for a well-aimed shot.

TWELVE

The side door of the theatre building opened and Corinna floated out on slippered feet. The wispy material of her costume fluttered around her knees as she came to stand beside the host. Her dark hair was pulled back into a sleek bun. Light glinted off something sparkly in her hair and the tight bodice of the leotard glittered with sequins and jewels.

The creamy white of her slender neck and gracefully sloped shoulders made her seem otherworldly compared to the big-haired, smartly dressed TV gal. Corinna's heavily made-up eyes and ruby-red lips emphasized her lovely cheekbones. Ben couldn't take his eyes off her. Affection for this beautiful woman expanded in his chest. The audience thundered with applause.

Corinna took the microphone and the clapping died down. "Good evening, everyone. Thank you for giving so generously to a worthwhile cause. The Miriam Shelter is a sanctuary for battered women and children. Our mission at the shelter is to stop domestic violence and to support families, by providing the essential tools for self-reliance through the delivery of emergency shelter, transitional housing, education, effective parenting education, and timely intervention with children and youth."

Earnestness rang in each word. Ben's respect grew. After all she'd been through with her father's death and being targeted herself, she could have hid away from the world. Not put herself out here to help others. It would have made his job easier if she hadn't been so strong, so brave. But then she wouldn't have been Corinna. The woman he'd fallen in love with.

"Your donations tonight and in the future will make the difference in many lives," she continued. "And there are many volunteer opportunities available."

Her expression softened. "I volunteer my time by giving dance lessons to the children. I can't express how much joy I receive from watching these kids blossom as they escape their circumstances for a short time through dance. It's a true blessing. Now I'd like to introduce Madame

Martin, the artistic director of the San Antonio Ballet Company."

Applause filled the air. Madame Martin glided out of the building and toward center stage.

The ear bud inside Ben's ear crackled. "We've got a commotion at point Bravo," Trevor said.

Point Bravo was on the other side of the theatre building. Adrenaline spiked in Ben's blood. "Jimenez?"

"No. Some other guy. I'll check out what's happening."

Just as Madame Martin took the microphone from Corinna, a man in jeans and a T-shirt came running from around the building and onto the stage heading straight for Corinna. Trevor and several uniformed SAPD officers rounded the building in hot pursuit.

Exclamations and gasps from onlookers echoed over the water. Madame Martin screamed. Corinna was left exposed when Addison scrambled back, but she didn't cower away. She stood her ground looking ready to fight.

Fear squeezed Ben's insides. He leapt into action, running toward the man and tackling him hard on the slick stage floor. The stench of alcohol gagged Ben as he flipped the guy onto his stomach, yanked the man's arms behind his back and secured his wrists with a knee to his spine. Ben took the handcuffs offered by an SAPD officer.

"Hey!" the man protested. "You gotta tell me where my wife is."

"Dude, I don't know anything about your wife," Ben growled and snapped the cuffs in place while helping Trevor haul the guy to his feet and off the stage. This was clearly not the show anyone came for and he had to get back to his spot to protect Corinna.

"She's at the Miriam Shelter! They gotta let me see her." The man bucked and fought.

Disdain filled Ben. The guy was obviously the drunken, abusive husband of one of the women at the shelter. "Take him away."

Two uniformed officers dragged the screaming man away.

"Sorry about that," Trevor said. "Guy sucker punched me."

Ben noticed the spot along Trevor's jaw that was now red but would soon darken into a nasty bruise. Tension mounted inside Ben but he held on to his anger. Greg had tried to coach Trevor often enough for Ben to know telling Trevor he should have been more alert wouldn't accomplish much. And the guy wondered why he'd been passed over for a promotion.

They needed to get moving and back into position. "Resume your post."

Trevor nodded and loped off and around to the back stage. Ben turned to Corinna. Her eyes were wide and her face pale. "You okay?"

She nodded. "A little shook up."

Madame Martin said something in Corinna's ear. Corinna nodded. "The show goes on," Madame stated.

Ben inclined his head and resumed his post.

Lifting the microphone, the older woman addressed the crowd, "Well, that was unexpected. But such is the world we live in, and our resolve is strengthened to assure the existence of safe havens such as Miriam's Shelter. Tonight you are in for a treat. Never performed before a live audience, I invite you to enjoy Pastiche, a ballet written and performed by the San Antonio Dance Company."

The lights went dark. Music filled the air.

A restless anticipation gripped Ben.

In the dim glow from the moon, he could see dancers taking their places. Slowly the stage lights rose, revealing an ensemble of twenty dancers. Corinna stood near the back of the group on the other side of the stage. They moved in unison to the music. Ben forced himself not to lose himself in Corinna's enchanting movements, but turned his attention to the crowd, searching for any suspicious actions.

When familiar music floated on the air, Ben couldn't help but focus on Corinna as she took centerstage along with her dance partner. Her fluid, graceful movements mesmerized Ben. A smile tugged at his mouth as his gaze followed her leaps across the stage.

Then a flash of light glinting off something to the left of the stage on the footbridge caught his eye. Heart racing, he stared hard at the spot on the bridge where he thought he'd seen something. Onlookers crowded along the ledge. He searched the people, trying to discern what had caught his attention.

Something wasn't right.

"Anderson, the footbridge," Ben said into his mic.

"Will do." Anderson's voice sounded in Ben's earpiece.

The hairs on the back of Ben's neck rose.

"Gun!" Anderson's voice shouted into Ben's ear.

Pedestrians screamed. Pandemonium broke out.

Ben didn't hesitate. He vaulted onto the stage

a second time and hurtled toward Corinna. He grabbed Corinna midleap and pushed her to the ground, covering her body with his just as the loud crack of a gun echoed off the brick bell arches. Searing pain blasted through Ben's side and spots of light exploded behind his eyelids. Corinna squirmed beneath him, shouting his name.

He wanted to reassure her she was safe, but the pain radiating from his side stole his breath and his words. All he could manage was a groan. He sent up a silent plea.

Don't let her be hurt, Lord.

The pinpricks of light winked out and blackness claimed him.

Terrified by the gun blast, Corinna pushed at Ben's heavy body. He didn't move. A horrifying thought crashed through her mind. He'd been shot.

"Ben!" she shouted. She squirmed, trying to move him off of her. He wouldn't budge. A sob tore from her.

"Please, dear God, don't let him die!"

The prayer was wrenched from her soul, releasing a floodgate of love and terror. She had never wanted to go to this horrible place of fear and grief again.

But she could no longer deny the emotion pressing on her heart, demanding to be acknowledged, to be released.

Aching warmth swept through her, filling every part of her being. She'd fallen in love with Ben.

Fallen in love with the goodness inside of him. The honor and integrity so innately a part of him. He was like her father, yet so much more. Ben was everything she could ever hope for in a man. Kind and caring. Loyal and brave.

And now he'd been shot. Her world set on the edge of collapse all over again.

Suddenly they were surrounded, and hands tugged at her, pulling her free. Ben was lifted away. Corinna saw the horror-filled gazes of the two Rangers who hadn't gone chasing after the shooter as they gathered around their captain. Tears burned her eyes.

Madame Martin's arms wrapped around Corinna. "Are you hurt?"

She shook her head. Not physically. But her heart had frozen with agonizing dread. She couldn't lose Ben, too. Regret that she hadn't told him of her feelings tumbled in her stomach.

Ben had been shot protecting her. Though she

couldn't see any blood, his head lolled back, his eyes closed.

EMTs pushed their way through the crowd, taking over Ben's care. They lifted his prone body to a rolling gurney.

Gisella stepped to Corinna's side. "We need to get you out of here."

The need to be with Ben gripped her. She shook her head. "I want to go with him."

"Not a good idea." Gisella took her arm. "I'll take you to the hospital. But for now I have to get you out of the open."

Watching Ben being rolled away ripped at Corinna's heart. He'd been her rock these past few weeks. Seeing him laid low was as right as a western sunrise.

Tears slipped down her cheeks as she allowed Gisella to whisk her back to the shelter of the theatre house. Once inside, Corinna sank down on a red velvet bench and yanked at the laces of her toe shoes and stripped off the footwear. She grabbed her dance bag and put on her tennis shoes. Gisella wore a path on the carpeted floor as she paced waiting for word that it was secure for them to move.

Corinna jumped to her feet and paced alongside Gisella.

He can't die. He can't die.

The words repeated through Corinna's mind.

God hasn't given up on you, so don't give up on Him. Ben's words wiped away her silent chanting.

Did she dare hope, trust that God would let Ben pull through this?

Her father's face rose in her mind. She could almost hear him say, *God will carry you through.* The same words he'd said to her after her mother died.

She'd lived in fear for so long, praying God would protect her father, yet her father was dead. Murdered. Now Ben was on his way to the hospital, shot by an assassin's bullet meant for her. It wasn't right, it wasn't fair.

Gisella touched her ear bud, clearly listening, then said, "On our way." She motioned for Corinna to follow her. "Let's go. A car is waiting."

Hurrying alongside the other woman, they left the building and rushed to a waiting black SUV. Daniel Riley sat in the driver's seat and Oliver Drew sat shotgun. Corinna slid into the backseat followed by Gisella.

As they rolled away from the theatre, Corinna said, "I want to go to the hospital."

From the driver's seat, Daniel replied, "That's where we're headed."

"Do you know...is...Ben...?"

Daniel exchanged a glance with Oliver. He shook his head. "Don't know."

Corinna sat back and stared unseeingly out the side window at the passing traffic. Desolation and despair pressed in on her. Fear slithered in. Would she find another loved one gone when she arrived at the hospital? Would evil win again?

Deep in her soul a welling tide of need rose, clogging her throat and burning her eyes. From some long forgotten Sunday school lesson came a verse that bolstered her downward spiraling faith.

For I know the plans I have for you, declares the Lord. Plans for good, not evil. To give you a future and a hope.

Closing her eyes, she breathed out a barely audible prayer. "If you really mean that, please don't let this evil destroy Ben."

Because she didn't think she could live through another loss of someone she loved.

At the hospital, Corinna was out of the vehicle before Daniel brought the SUV to a full stop. Oliver quickly followed. An empty ambulance sat at the emergency entrance. Corinna hurried through the sliding doors and rushed to the admitting desk.

A gray-haired lady sitting behind the counter smiled at her. "How can I help you?"

"Ben Fritz. He was just brought in," Corinna nearly gasped.

The older woman's fingers played across the keyboard of the computer in front of her. Her brow wrinkled in a frown. "I'm sorry, I don't see anyone in our system with that name."

"But he just came in," Corinna insisted. "He was shot. He should be back with the doctors."

"I'm sorry, Miss. I have no record of him."

"The ambulance is here," Oliver interjected. "Where are the EMTs?" Without waiting for an answer, Oliver peeled away from the counter and headed toward the ER doors.

"Hey, you can't go in there!" A nurse ran after him.

Confusion and alarm squeezed Corinna's lungs, trapping her breath. "How can that be?"

Daniel and Gisella raced to her side just as Oliver returned. "He's not here," Oliver stated. "EMTs said as soon as he regained consciousness he took off."

Their shocked faces reflected the question burning through her mind. Where could he be?

* * *

"I can't believe I let you talk me into this!" Anderson said with a sideways glance while expertly handling his truck at a breakneck speed.

Ben tried not wincing every time the vehicle rounded a corner or hit a rough patch of road in their pursuit of the shooter. "Wasn't like I gave you a choice. It was an order."

"Dumb one, if you ask me," Anderson groused.

"Not when the order leads to catching this guy. That's all that matters," Ben stated firmly through clenched teeth.

His broken rib burned like a roaring campfire gone awry. When he'd come to in the back of the ambulance before the vehicle had left the Riverwalk, the EMTs had told him his Kevlar vest had stopped the bullet, but he'd suffered a rib fracture and they wanted to take him to the hospital for x-rays. They'd strapped tape around his midsection and instructed him to take full breaths to avoid lung complications.

They'd also wanted to start him on pain meds, but Ben had refused. It was bad enough he'd passed out. He needed a clear head, especially when he saw Jimenez running toward the parking garage. He'd been surprised to see him still so close. Jimenez must have hunkered down somewhere hoping to escape when the police presence diminished.

Though the EMTs had argued with Ben when he'd demanded to be released from the gurney to go chase after Jimenez, he'd prevailed, promising he'd go have an x-ray as soon as he could. He had something more important to do.

A shudder ripped through him, eliciting a hiss of pain, as he remembered how close that bullet had come to hitting Corinna. He was gratified he'd managed to get to Corinna in time to save her. It was his job to capture the creep after her, but he also wanted to give her peace. He didn't want her living in fear as a target anymore. She deserved to live her life free from this threat.

And Ben would do anything to make that happen.

He just had to bring the guy down and put him behind bars.

When his quarry had pulled out of the garage in a red compact car and roared away, Ben and Anderson wasted precious seconds arguing, until Ben had pulled rank. They'd hustled as fast as Ben's injury would allow to Anderson's truck.

Now they followed after Jimenez. And this time, Ben was determined the monster would not get away.

"Drop back a bit," Ben instructed. "Don't want him to notice us."

Anderson eased up on the gas and changed lanes behind a minivan. They followed Jimenez down I-37, keeping a couple of car lengths between them. When Jimenez exited, they did the same, taking the off-ramp toward the Alamodome. The traffic became more congested the closer they drew to the sports arena. Ben thought for a moment they'd been made when Jimenez abruptly took a right turn.

Anderson shot past the street. "Did he make us?"

Ignoring the pulling pain in his side, Ben craned his head to watch Jimenez. "Don't think so. He pulled into the hotel parking lot."

Anderson drove them around the block and doubled back. Pulling his truck to the curb, they watched Jimenez scurry from his vehicle toward the hotel building, disappearing inside.

"You call for back up," Ben said opening the door. "I'll see where he went."

"Wait! You—"

Ben shut the door, cutting off Anderson's protest.

The driver's door jerked open and Anderson jumped out of the truck. "Dude, don't go all Lone Ranger on me. I'm not losing another captain."

Ben flinched at the reminder of the way Greg had died. Alone. Because he hadn't kept them in the loop. Inclining his head, Ben said, "Make the call. Then we go in. Together."

With a grunt that was somewhere between satisfaction and acceptance, Anderson made the call to Cade, then turned to Ben. "He's on his way. He'll let the others know."

Biting the inside of his cheek against the pain of his burning side, Ben hustled alongside Anderson, down the street and entered the lobby of the cheap motel. Orange carpeting and fake wood paneling hurtled Ben back to the seventies. The stale odor of cigarettes assaulted Ben's nose, burning the already tender flesh. Amazing how a busted nose made his sense of smell more sensitive.

A teenage kid with ear buds attached to an iPod sat behind the counter, reading. His greasy hair didn't move as his head bobbed in time to whatever music he listened to. The kid's gaze was glued to the book lying face up on the Formica countertop.

Refusing to let his pain hinder him, Ben stalked to the desk and waved a hand in front of the kid's face. The kid jerked back, his hands taking the ear buds out, while his expression turned from surprised annoyance to fear when his gaze landed on the star pinned to Ben's chest.

"Ranger Fritz," Ben announced as he pulled a copy of the sketch from his breast pocket and held it up. "We need to know which room Eddie Jimenez has."

The kid swallowed and his pronounced Adam's apple bobbled. "I'm not supposed to give out that kind of information."

Anderson sidled up. "Look, we can drag your sorry hide in for obstruction of justice or you can give us the room number and you get left alone."

The kid's gaze darted back and forth between them as he clearly weighed his options. With a shrug, he hopped off his stool and moved to the computer. With quick strokes he brought up the hotel registry and turned the monitor around so Ben could see the screen.

A smile of satisfaction tightened Ben's mouth. "Got an extra key for Room 303?"

"I can make one," the kid said, already reaching for a plastic keycard. With a few keystrokes and a swipe through the encoder system, the kid handed over the keyless entry into Jimenez's room.

Ben tipped his hat. "Much obliged."

With Anderson at his heels, Ben prowled toward Room 303. He stopped at the door and withdrew his sidearm.

Anderson mirrored him as he whispered, "Shouldn't we wait?"

Giving a negative shake of his head, Ben readied himself.

Holding up three fingers to indicate they'd move on three, Ben counted down. On the final count, he swiped the card. Anderson turned the knob and pushed the door open. Ben entered the room, the pain streaking through his right side screaming as he aimed his weapon at the man scrambling from the bed.

"Don't move," Ben shouted. "Hands where I can see them."

Jimenez froze, his wild-eyed gaze jumping between Ben and Anderson. Slowly, he raised his arms. "Am I under arrest?"

"Have you done something we need to arrest you for?" Anderson stalked forward and patted Jimenez down while Ben kept his weapon steadily trained on the perp's forehead. "We're taking you in for questioning in the attempted murder of a Texas Ranger."

Ben realized what Anderson was doing. As long as they didn't formally arrest Jimenez, they didn't have to read him his Miranda rights and anything the guy spontaneously said would be admissible in court.

Anderson cuffed the guy. Holding on to Jimenez's arm, Anderson's gaze moved to something over Ben's shoulder, his eyes widening. "Turn around," he said to Ben.

Ben whipped around to find himself staring at a collage of photos, starring Corinna, thumb-tacked to the wall. The images were candid photos taken from a distance. Coming and going from Gisella's house, from the studio and even some outside the shelter. Newspaper clippings of Greg's death and the memorial announcement were taped beside the pictures.

Fury exploded in Ben's gut, pushing all pain and legalities of his job aside. Had Greg died because this guy had a fixation on his daughter? But where did coma guy fit in? And why was the sicko out to kill the target of his obsession?

In a swift move, Ben holstered his weapon and pounced on Jimenez, roughly grabbing him by the throat, ripping him out of Anderson's grasp and forcing him backward.

"Why?" Ben roared.

Jimenez shook, fear twisting his face. "What?"

"Why are you trying to kill Corinna Pike? Why did you kill her father?"

Sweat beaded on Jimenez's brow. "What are you talking about?"

"You killed Greg Pike."

Jimenez looked between the two men, his eyes wide with fear. "No. That wasn't me. I—"

"You're going down."

Shaking his head, Jimenez said, "I didn't kill her father."

The sound of sirens bounced off the cheap hotel room walls.

Ben tightened his hold, squeezing Jimenez's windpipe. "Why are you trying to kill Corinna?"

Jimenez glanced at the wall of photos. He swallowed, his Adam's apple scraping across Ben's palm.

"Tell me!" Ben snarled. "Or I end you here and now."

"You can't! You're the law."

Ben moved in close until his face was a hairs-breadth from Jimenez's. "Today I'm not."

"Ben," Anderson interjected close to Ben's ear. "We've got company. Let him go. We'll interrogate him at the station."

"No. I want answers now!" Ben's fingers flexed.

Jimenez's face turned red as his air supply diminished. Something in Ben's eyes must have convinced Eddie Jimenez his life span was rapidly narrowing. "She saw me," Jimenez choked out. "Could ID me."

"Let me read him his rights," Anderson ground out.

Even though Ben wanted nothing more than to choke the life out of the creep in front of him, his rational side sprang to life and shoved through anger's haze. He couldn't jeopardize the case by not Mirandizing Jimenez. His admission was already at risk. Ben was stunned by the depth of fury pumping through his veins. Nor could he believe how close he'd come to crossing the line between good and evil.

All because he'd let himself fall in love with the person he was supposed to be protecting. Loving Corinna put Ben's whole world at risk. If he kept on this course of action, Corinna would become his Achilles' heel, his vulnerable spot.

Ben suddenly appreciated Greg's determination to keep his daughter as isolated from his life as possible. Ben would have to follow suit.

Giving one final squeeze to Jimenez, Ben abruptly let go. Jimenez staggered. Anderson grabbed the guy by the arm and dragged him out of the hotel room.

Ben took one final glance at the wall of pictures. Rage shuddered through him. He was going to nail Jimenez to the wall. For himself, for Greg. For Corinna.

"Are you out of your mind?" Corinna shouted at Ben, preventing him from entering the interrogation room where Jimenez was being held. Fear for what he'd done and relief that he was all right mingled to create a confusing jumble inside of her, making her upset over the events of the evening even more intense.

She'd been with Daniel and Gisella when they received the call informing them that Ben and Anderson had tracked the suspect to a hotel, instead of going to the hospital. Daniel and Oliver had taken off, leaving Gisella and Corinna to wait at the hospital for a taxi. When news came that the shooter had been apprehended and taken to the SAPD, Corinna had convinced Gisella they needed to go to the station. Corinna had needed to assure herself that Ben was alive and safe.

From the moment she arrived at the station, she'd been hounding the Rangers to let her talk to him. Now that she had him in front of her, her outrage at his lack of common sense for running after the bad guy while injured cooled.

Ben was ashen, making the dark bruises around his nose more pronounced. Her heart ached for him but at the same time she was angry. Though she couldn't see the bandages wrapped around his side, the singed hole on his shirt made her shudder. It could have killed him. She remembered her own searing pain when she'd been merely grazed by a bullet. She was just so thankful he'd had on his bullet-proof vest.

"Corinna, not now. I've got to question Jimenez."

Though Ben's voice was gentle, she could hear the tension in the undertones. Empathy for the pain he had to be feeling arced through her. "Let someone else question him. You need to see a doctor."

"I'm fine. The EMTs patched me up."

He didn't look fine. She reached out to touch

his arm. She'd lost her father. She couldn't lose Ben, too. "Sit, before you collapse and hurt yourself more."

His hazel eyes narrowed and his jaw worked. "I'm not going to collapse. I've got a job to do."

"You already did your job."

"I have to see it through to the end."

The door to the interrogation room opened. Anderson stepped into the doorway. "You coming?"

"Yeah." Ben covered her hand on his arm. "Go home with Gisella."

She shook her head, unwilling to leave him even for a moment. She loved this man and would make sure he took care of himself. That was her job. "No. I'll wait here."

He swiped a hand over his face. "This might take a long time. I need you to go. Please. I can't deal with you right now."

Stung by his last sentence, she shook her head. "I don't care how long it takes. I'll stay."

His expression hardened. "There's no reason for you to. You're safe now."

Her fist clenched. Stubborn man. "I know I'm safe. It's you I'm worried about. I want to make sure you're all right."

His eyebrows pulled together. "I'm not your concern."

"But you and I—"

He cut her off. "There is no you and I. We're done."

Taken aback, she blinked. *We're done.* Misery hit her between the eyes. He couldn't be any clearer. She'd been a job. A promise kept. Nothing more. He had his bad guy and she was dismissed.

Hoping her expression didn't give away the anguish burrowing deep into her heart, she turned and walked away.

Obviously, her concern wasn't wanted or appreciated. She doubted her love would be, either. Good thing she hadn't confessed her deeper feelings to Ben. The last thing she needed right now was rejection.

How could she have been so stupid not to see more clearly?

Being a Ranger came first. It always had with her father. It always would with Ben.

But Ben…

Pain seared her soul.

She'd thought this was…different, special.

But it wasn't. She wasn't.

She was just another case. Just another victim.

Time for him to move on to the next hapless soul who needed his help.

Tears stung her eyes, but she refused to let them fall.

She'd just have to learn to live without Ben.

THIRTEEN

Ben watched Corinna march away. There'd been no mistaking the hurt in her pretty dark eyes. He couldn't help that now. He hadn't meant to be short with her or so blunt. Pain from his busted rib and the anger smoldering near the surface were hard enough to control. He just hadn't the strength to confront her concern or expound upon the knowledge that loving her put them both at risk.

It tore him up inside that he couldn't tell her he loved her, but she would be better off without that information because a relationship between them wasn't possible.

Desolation spread through him. He didn't belong with her. Never had and never would. He'd only taint her life with the evil he dealt with every day and put her, himself and his team at risk.

If Ben were to allow a relationship with Corinna

to develop to something lasting, there wouldn't be any way to keep her safe. And she deserved to be safe. She deserved so much more than him.

Feeling hollow inside, he forced her from his mind. He entered the square utilitarian interrogation room. Eddie Jimenez sat in a metal folding chair, his hands cuffed to the metal table. A pad of paper and a pen lay off to one side. Purple bruises marred the olive skin covering his throat. Ben had come as close as he'd ever had to wanting to take another life.

Disappointment for losing control ate him up, making him feel ten years old. He could only imagine how disappointed God must be with him right now.

Anderson leaned against the wall, his arms crossed over his massive chest. He made an intimidating presence. Ben gave the Ranger a nod before he pulled out the chair opposite Jimenez and sat down.

"So tell me, why did you kill Greg Pike?" Ben said.

Jimenez frowned. "I told you, man. I didn't kill him. And I don't know who did."

"I don't believe you," Ben stated, keeping his voice even. He had to play this cool; he didn't want to get Eddie too wound up, then he'd be asking for a lawyer that Ben wasn't going to offer. "What happened? You became obsessed with his daughter and he found out?"

Jimenez shook his head. "No. You got it all wrong."

"Then enlighten me," Ben said.

When Jimenez stayed silent, Ben said, "The killing of a Ranger is a capital offense. You know what that means, right?"

Ben leaned in closer. "Lethal injection."

Jimenez flinched. Beads of sweat dripped down the sides of his face. He licked his lips. "I never met Pike," he stated, his voice raising an octave.

"Until you killed him."

"No, man. I promise. I'll take a lie detector test and everything."

Ben sat back digesting the offer. The test wouldn't be admissible if he didn't pass. But would still be damaging. Would Jimenez really submit to taking a lie detector test if he had killed Greg? He didn't think so. "Why did you try to kill Corinna Pike?"

Jimenez's gaze dropped to his hands. Silence stretched.

Ben decided to yank Eddie's chain. He pushed back his chair, the metal legs scraping on the concrete floor making a hideous sound. "Too bad, Eddie. I guess it's the needle for you."

Jimenez's chin jerked up, his eyes flashed with panic. "Hey, no. I'm telling you, I didn't kill no Ranger. I was hired to do a job. That's all. The girl saw me. I couldn't let her ID me. But I didn't kill anyone."

Alarms went off in Ben's head. "Hired? By who and for what?"

Horror flooded Jimenez's face. "No one. I don't know."

Interesting. He was more afraid of the person who hired him than he was of jail time. Ben resumed his seat. "Come on, Eddie. It will go a lot better for you with the DA if you cooperate."

Ben leaned back as if they were having a relaxing conversation. The posture was to put Jimenez at ease and hopefully make him feel more inclined to talk. "What were you looking for in the Pike house?"

Jimenez once again dropped his gaze to the table.

"Eddie. Eddie, come on." Ben bent his head trying to make eye contact. "Did the Lions of Texas put you up to this?"

Jimenez's body jerked and his eyes widened with terror. Ben's shot in the dark hit pay dirt.

"Tell me about the Lions of Texas. Are they a gang related to La Eme?"

Jimenez blinked then barked out a laugh. "No."

Frowning, Ben said, "Then what?"

Turning his head away, Eddie didn't say anything.

Remembering the rap sheet he'd read on Eddie, Ben threw out, "Is this your drug cartel?"

"Not mine," Eddie said, then clamped his mouth tight with a stricken expression.

"So the Lions of Texas are running drugs." Ben exchanged a glance with Anderson. "That's a long way from murder, Eddie. Could be good for you, if you cooperate."

When he didn't reply, Ben slammed his palms on the table. Jimenez jumped. "Who's in charge?"

"I don't know," Eddie mumbled. "I'm too low. I was just hired to see if there was anything incriminating on the Lions in Pike's house. That's all I was doing. When the girl saw me, I knew the Lions would kill me if I didn't silence her."

A blast of anger blew through Ben, but he maintained his composure. "So who hired you? Come on, I'll put in a good word with the DA if you give me a name."

"I don't have a name. That's not how it works," Eddie said.

"Okay. Then how *does* it work?"

Eddie swallowed, hard. "Man, they'll kill me if I say anything more. I took an oath."

"You'll get the death penalty if you go away for Pike's murder," Ben stated, watching the words sink in. "Right now, I'm the only one who believes you didn't kill him."

"This ain't right. I didn't kill him."

"I know. But, hey." Ben held his hands out, palms up as if to say "sorry." "You gotta give me something to take to the DA."

A tick formed near Jimenez's right eye. "I don't know anything."

"You said you swore an oath. What kind of oath? And to whom?"

"I never saw them. I was blindfolded."

"That's putting a lot of trust in someone you don't know, Eddie. A little unbelievable."

Jimenez shrugged. "I swore to support the Lions of Texas in their bid to open the Mexican borders. They pay me well."

Ben leaned in with horror running roughshod over his anger. "Human trafficking?"

"Naw, man. Like you said, drugs. *Llello.* White gold. Cocaine."

Ben sat back. On the one hand he was glad this wasn't about human cargo. He didn't even want to contemplate the various ways that scenario could play out. Yet, on the other hand... drugs. The bane of every law enforcement agency across the country. The war on drugs was a drain on society.

His fist clenched at his sides. And the Lions of Texas wanted to bring the poison in freely across the borders, infiltrating the schools and neighborhoods of America. Ripping more lives apart. Destroying families. "How were you contacted?"

Eddie blew out a breath. "You gonna protect me?"

Shooting another glance at Anderson and seeing in his eyes the same excitement at how close they were getting, Ben said, "We'll protect you."

Jimenez assessed Ben for a moment before saying, "I picked up my instructions at a drop site. I don't see anyone and I don't talk to no one."

Shoving the pad and pen so that Eddie could use them, Ben said, "Write down the directions."

Picking up the pen, Eddie paused. "You'll talk to the DA. Tell him I didn't kill anyone."

"Is Corinna Pike still in danger?" Ben countered.

Jimenez pulled a face. "Naw. No reason for anyone to go after her now. I'm the only one she can identify. And that ship has long sailed."

The weight of worry lifted off Ben's shoulders, making him feel lightheaded. Corinna was safe. No one was coming after her again.

"Yeah, sure, I'll talk to the DA." Ben's lip curled. He'd make sure the creep went to prison for a very long time.

A knock at the door brought Ben to his feet. Anderson opened the door and Daniel waved them out into the hall.

From the excited light in the Ranger's eyes, Ben hoped they'd had a break in the case. Anticipation mounted.

"A man called saying he'd seen coma guy's picture on the television. Says he saw him out by some animal rescue center up I-10 between here and Austin," Daniel said.

"Get the witness down here," Ben ordered.

"Already sent Oliver and Marvel to pick him up."

"Good job."

Ben motioned for the two Rangers to follow him back into the interrogation room. "You know anything about an animal rescue center?" Ben asked.

"Hey, that's here," Eddie said, stabbing the pad of paper with the pen indicating the directions he'd just written out. "Rodger's Exotic Animal Rescue Farm."

Ben didn't believe in coincidence. The Lions of Texas and Captain Pike's murder were connected. Greg must have discovered the organization and its operation. Now if they could just figure out how coma guy fit in and who was behind the Lions of Texas....

Energized by this new development, Ben motioned the Rangers back into the hall and closed the door to the interrogation room.

"Somehow this animal rescue center plays a part in Greg's murder and the Lions of Texas. We need to keep Eddie under wraps so he can't warn anyone off the site." Ben's mind raced. "Anderson, you up for a little covert operation?"

The big blond Ranger grinned. "You bet."

With an approving nod, Ben said, "Find out everything you can about this animal rescue center and its employees. Someone there's got to be involved. And whoever it is, I want them taken down." Turning to Daniel, Ben said, "Help Anderson with his cover. I'll call the Governor and the DEA. We've got to get ahead of this."

"Will do," Daniel said.

The two men turned in unison and stalked away. Ben had every faith that they would soon find the answers to the mystery of Greg's murder. His team wouldn't rest until the case was closed. No matter how long it took.

If only he were as confident about his relationship with Corinna. Unfortunately, it wasn't a mystery. His and Corinna's relationship was going nowhere.

Saturday morning rushed at Corinna, just as it had done every day for the past week. Now that she was no longer in danger, she and Gabby had moved back into the Pike family house and were readjusting to being home. Most of her days were spent either at the shelter or the dance studio and every night, she paced the rooms of her lonely house, alternating between missing Ben and being angry at him.

She'd told herself to let go of her feelings for Ben and her dreams of a future with him. He'd made his feelings clear. He didn't want her. It was time to move forward with her life.

Except her heart was broken.

But what could she do?

Healing would come with time. Surprisingly, she'd found comfort in her Bible and in prayer. But loneliness seemed to be a constant companion.

The door bell rang. For a split second her heart jumped. Ben? Had he remembered they'd made a date for today?

Quickly, she squelched the thought. Ben wouldn't be coming over ever again. She knew who was at the door. Gisella had called to say she was stopping by on her way to the gym. Their friendship had blossomed while Corinna had lived with the Ranger. Corinna jerked the door open. "Hi. Come in."

"You okay? You don't look too good," Gisella said as she entered the house. She wore jersey shorts over a bright multi-colored racerback swim suit. Her dark hair was pulled tightly back into a braid. Her flipflops slapped against the hardwood as she followed Corinna to the kitchen.

"How long does a broken heart take to heal?" Corinna muttered as she moved to the coffee maker and poured the hot liquid into two mugs.

She'd confided in Gisella of her feelings for Ben and then promptly swore her to secrecy.

Gisella had made excuses for Ben, saying he'd been stressed and hadn't meant what he'd said. The man had just been shot, was trying to solve a murder and had been angry that Jimenez had gotten so close to Corinna.

Corinna would have liked to give him the benefit of the doubt. Except she was too afraid to let her hope rise. More heartache lay down that path.

Frowning, Gisella took the mug of coffee. "You really should try to talk to him again. Now that things have settled down some."

"No. I know the score. Now that he doesn't have to protect me anymore, he doesn't want to have anything to do with me."

She couldn't help the self-pity worming its way through her. She'd lost so much in the past month. Her father. Now Ben. She mentally scoffed. She never had Ben to begin with. And who's fault was that?

Her own. She hadn't told him how she felt, though she doubted it would have made much difference. His feelings for her were set long before her father's death. Ben had been in her life for over a decade and she'd never given him the time of day, until she'd needed him. How selfish and self-absorbed she'd been.

She'd been told often over the years that she was cold and closed off. He probably saw that as well. Could she really blame him for not wanting her? He'd fulfilled his promise to her father. He was done. He'd said as much.

She really should let go of her love for him. Just move on with her life. She would do fine without love.

The problem was she didn't want to go forward without Ben. She loved him and longed for him to love her back.

She could think of a very good reason why a future with him seemed ludicrous. He lived a life of danger. Just like her father. She'd vowed to leave that world behind.

Did she really want to put herself at risk of going through that kind of agony again? Could she survive the death of another person she loved?

God hasn't given up on you, so don't give up on Him.

Her hand tightened on the mug. Did she dare trust God enough to take the risk?

Gisella's hand on her shoulder drew her out of her thoughts. "You know, I've always lived by the adage that if something is worth loving then it's worth fighting for."

Arching an eyebrow, Corinna stared. "You think I should fight for Ben's love?"

Mirroring Corinna, Gisella arched an eyebrow. "*Do* you love him?"

Suddenly finding swallowing difficult, Corinna slowly nodded. She did love Ben. With her whole heart.

Gisella grinned. "Then you know what you have to do."

"But I'm afraid."

"That he'll reject you?"

Breathing deep and then letting the air out through pursed lips, Corinna said, "Partly."

"And the other part?"

How did she explain to this woman who lived the same risky life? "How do you do it? How do you do this job knowing how dangerous it is?"

Dawning entered Gisella's eyes. "I see." She moved to the counter, her gaze taking on a far-away look as if remembering something that made her sad. "I do this because I want to make a difference."

Turning to fully face Corinna, she said, "And yeah, it's not safe. But life isn't always safe. Or easy. Or simple. I'm careful and I depend on God." She shrugged. "That's all any of us can do."

She pinned Corinna with a pointed look. "You just have to decide for yourself. Do you want to play it safe and live without love? Or is love worth the risk of facing an uncertain future?"

Gisella set her mug in the sink. "Search your heart, Corinna. Ask God. Only you can make that choice."

With those words hanging in the air, Gisella walked out the front door. Alone, Corinna turned to stare out the kitchen window at the blue, cloudless sky. Her heart galloped like wild horses spooked by a rattler. Could she risk it all? Was her love for Ben big enough, strong enough, was her faith deep enough?

Dredging up faith from the far reaches of her soul, she lifted her voice toward Heaven. "I do love him. But God, I'm so afraid."

She had a choice to make. Could she accept the risk in choosing Ben?

Only one way to find out.

Sunday morning the echo of a knock jerked Ben awake from a restless dream, reliving the moment on the stage when Jimenez took his shot. Sharp, stabbing pain in his side took his breath away.

Only in the dream, it was Corinna who'd taken the bullet. A residual shudder of horror rocked through him as the remnants of the nightmare left to be replaced with reality.

He breathed in, filling his lungs as much as the pain would allow. Sunlight streamed through the skylight overhead, bathing him in warmth.

Sitting up, Ben pushed the sheet back and let out a wry scoff. He'd fallen into bed at 3:00 a.m. in his clothes. He glanced at the clock. Almost 10:00 a.m. Scrubbing a hand over his face, he told himself he'd have to thank Cade Jarvis for insisting he head home for some sleep. Obviously, he'd needed it.

But he had to get back to work. Anderson would be going undercover on Monday and there was still so much to put in place beforehand. He sensed they had a long way to go to crack the case, but each clue brought them closer to the Lions and Greg's killer.

The sound of the front door opening and closing echoed through the quiet apartment.

His heart stalled. Only one person had a key to his apartment. Corinna.

Knowing the time had come to face the inevitable, he gingerly rose from the bed and padded down the hall in his stocking feet.

Corinna stood frozen in the middle of the living room hugging her purse like a shield. She was a vision in a soft pink dress that hugged her curves in all the right places and flirted with her knees, exposing her well-defined calves and slender ankles. Open-toed silver sandals revealed pink polish on her toes. She'd left her shoulder length hair down and flowing over her creamy shoulders exposed by the thin straps of her dress.

Her expression of uncertainty hit him like a sledgehammer, reminding him how fragile and vulnerable she was. Then her dark eyes flashed with anger and something else…relief or resolve? He wasn't sure.

"Hi," he said inanely.

"Hi, yourself. Hope you don't mind that I let myself in. I wasn't sure you were here so I was going to leave you this," she said, pulling an envelope, the kind that housed a card, from her purse.

"That's fine." A knot of dread bunched up in his stomach. What had she written on the card? He held out his hand for the envelope.

She hesitated. "I guess since I'm here, I don't really need to give this to you."

Code for she wanted to talk. The living room

seemed suddenly too small for the two of them, too close. "I'll make us some coffee."

He edged past her to go to the safety of the kitchen. He caught a whiff of Corinna's citrusy scent and fought the urge to pull her close and bury his nose in her hair.

"I've already had some, thanks," she said following him, blocking the exit. For such a petite woman, she made a formidable barrier.

"I haven't." He made quick work of starting the Brew Master.

When the machine gurgled and began spitting out dark java, he turned to face her. Wretchedness stabbed at him. The torment of her presence squeezed the air from his lungs. He'd tried so hard to stay away these past few days, hoping that time and distance would help them both realize the crazy attraction and emotional connection zinging between them was born out of crisis and grief and not something that could last.

But he was lying to himself.

And having her right in front of him, her gaze devouring him like she hadn't eaten in a week, made his resolve to do the honorable thing by denying his feelings crack. But not break. He had to stay strong and not let himself give over to the love in his heart.

"Why didn't you return my call yesterday?"

He blew out a breath. "It's been a crazy time. We've got a lot going on."

"Are you any closer to finding my father's killer?"

"We're on his trail. Anderson is going undercover to track down a good lead. Don't worry though, I won't rest until we have the person responsible for Greg's death."

"I know you won't," she replied, her voice holding a note of admiration. "Gisella told me you all are sure I'm no longer a target."

"That's true. Jimenez agreed to a polygraph test and passed. He was the only one after you. Now that he's in jail for attempted murder, you've nothing left to fear. I'm sorry I didn't tell you myself."

Her eyes narrowed as she considered his apology. "You can make it up to me."

Mild surprise flickered. He arched an eyebrow. "Oh. How?"

She leaned a hip against the counter, relaxing slightly. "Well, first by going to church with me this morning."

He blinked. "Church?" What day was it? He'd been working so much he hadn't even realized... "You want to go to church?"

A soft smile touched her lush lips. "Yes. I figure I'm going to need my faith if I'm going to get what I want."

Anticipation sizzled along his nerve endings. "Okay. Sounds a bit odd."

She gave a delicate shrug. "The Bible says *Delight yourself in the Lord and He will give you the desires of your heart.* I'm choosing to believe Him."

"I don't think that verse means God will grant you any wish you want, but rather He'll put the right desires in your heart."

A beaming smile lit her face, making his toes curl.

"Then it's true," she said. "Because my desire goes against logic and reason. Therefore, He must have given it to me, right?"

He tried to sort out her words and found them as clear as the mud at the bottom of the Rio Grande. "I haven't a clue what you're talking about."

She giggled, a pleasing sound that strummed his senses. A tremor of pure attraction shuddered through him. He sucked in a sharp breath.

When she smoothly advanced on him, he found himself cornered, his back literally against the wall. His palms began to sweat. Emotions bounced around his chest like pinballs.

She laid a warm, delicate hand on his chest. "What I want, Ranger Fritz, is you."

Sure he hadn't heard her right, Ben stuck a finger in his ear and shook it as if to make his hearing better. She couldn't have just said she wanted him. Him? His pulse beat at sonic speed and his temperature skyrocketed through the roof. "Excuse me. What did you say?"

The edges of her mouth tipped upward in a coy smile. "You heard me."

Who was this vibrant and determined woman in front of him? Gone was any trace of the icy aloofness he used to receive from her. This was no fragile ballerina needing to be coddled and protected. He'd seen glimpses of this woman over the past month but now…wow. His mind exploded, sending him off balance. And the love he'd already acknowledged detonated within him, filling every fiber of his being. He fought to breathe, to think.

"I did hear you. And it's out of the question for so many reasons."

Clamping his hands on her upper arms, though careful not to touch the tender welt from the bullet grazing, he lifted her slightly off her feet and set her aside so he could move past her without knocking her over.

She dogged his steps into the living room. "How can you say that?"

Needing air, he opened the sliding glass door. The happy sounds of the children who lived in the apartment complex playing outside stirred a painful yearning in his soul. He shut the sliding glass door, blocking out the sounds of his deepest desire. A family to belong to. He had a family. The Rangers were his family.

Anything else... He couldn't.

Keeping his back to her, he said, "I can't. You and me, well, a relationship between us wouldn't be right."

"You can't? Not right?"

The confusion and outrage in her voice stabbed at him. His resolve faltered, but he stayed the course for her sake, as well as his. He never broke a promise.

Turning, he steeled himself to meet her gaze. She deserved the respect. "I made a promise to your father to watch out for you."

Her face showed confusion. "And you did. Admirably. You saved my life, you caught the bad guy and put him in jail. What more could anyone ask?"

Anguish clogged his throat barely letting the words pass.

"You don't understand. The promise was more encompassing than that. Your father wanted more for you. I want more for you."

"More?" She made a face. "You're right. I don't understand. What *more* could there be?"

He ran a hand through his hair. "A good life. A safe life. A life without all the baggage that comes with…my world."

An indignant light entered her dark gaze. She held up a hand. "Hold up! Wait a sec. You don't get to decide what kind of life I need." She pointed to herself. "I get to. And I've lived in your world my whole life."

"Not really. Your father kept you insulated. He didn't ever want to put you at risk. And I don't either."

She cut the air with her hand in a slicing motion. "Do you think I haven't thought this through? Do you think I haven't told myself that I should walk away from the pain and sorrow that is inherent with the life of a Ranger?"

She advanced on him. "A wise woman told me life isn't safe. I know that. Ben, I don't want safe. I want…" Suddenly, she hesitated as insecurity flashed across her face. She took a deep breath and slowly exhaled. "Tell me you don't feel anything for me and I'll walk away. I'll leave you to your life."

His mouth was as dry as cotton. Her words scorched a trail to his heart. He couldn't tell her he didn't feel anything. He would be lying. He loved her. The words sat on his tongue but refused to let go.

"Look," Ben said. "You don't know what you're saying. What you're asking. You deserve so much more than the likes of me. I can't let you settle."

Frustration crossed her face as she shook her head. "Not your call."

He had to make her see reason. "Your feelings are born out of grief. They won't last. You need time to figure out what you really want in life. This has been an intense month. You've lost your father. You've been shot and shot at. Your world has been turned upside down. You've changed—"

"No. I haven't changed." She stepped closer. "But I've grown. I finally feel like I can be *me*. There's no more anger and resentment holding me down. I do know what I want in life. Time isn't going to change that. And yes, it's been an intense month. We've both suffered a great loss." Tears filled her eyes. "My world imploded. But

I survived, not only physically, but emotionally and spiritually, because of you."

"But that doesn't mean you…" He couldn't bring himself to say the word love. He couldn't hope her feelings were real. If he allowed her fully into his heart and then she left…he didn't want to go down that awful road again.

"Yes, it does." She wrapped her arms around his waist and leaned back to look up into his face. "I love you."

Everything inside him stilled. Joy blasted through him. He tamped it down. Slowly, he extracted himself from her embrace.

"You deserve so much better than me. You should have a life that doesn't put your safety at risk."

She shook her head with a determined gleam in her eyes. "You don't get to make that judgment. That's a decision only I get to make. And I choose you."

"You don't understand." He ran a hand through his hair. "Loving me puts you in danger. Puts me in danger. And my team. If someone wanted to get at me, all they would have to do is go after you. I can't live with that."

"That's ridiculous." Her expression hardened with determination. "If every law enforcement officer thought that way none of them would marry and have kids. Besides, aren't you the one who told me God is good? If you really believed that, then you'd trust God with us. Where's your faith, Ben?"

Her words sliced through him like a knife carving through butter. She was right. If he really believed, really had faith that God worked in his life, then he'd have the faith to trust that God would protect them both. "I do have enough faith in God. I just don't have faith in love."

Her eyebrows drew together. "I don't understand."

"How long will your love last?"

"Forever."

"You say that now." He swiped a hand over his face, feeling exposed and raw as he let out his deepest fear. "Your love will wane and then you'll regret your decision and…leave."

For a long moment she stared. "Not going to happen. Once I commit, I'm fully committed. Love as an emotion, a feeling…" She shrugged. "Yeah, it will ebb and flow just as all emotions and feelings do. That's part of being human. That will have no bearing on my commitment. And I am ready to leap, jump, dive into a relationship with you, Ben. You and only you."

He so desperately wanted to believe her words. "But—"

"No buts." Her expression gentled. Compassion filled her pretty eyes. "I get it. This is a lot to take in. And it's out of the blue. And we don't really know each other." She made a face. "I mean, we've known each other for a long time, but we don't *really* know each other. We can go slow. Take our time figuring this out. Whatever you want. But I'm in. All the way."

Her words zoomed straight to his heart. All in. If she were willing to take the risk of loving him, could he do no less?

They stared at each for a long moment. A slow smile spread through him. The depth of love shining in her eyes wouldn't be denied. She loved him. Him.

"I love you, too." The words burst from his mouth like a dam breaking. In a swift move, he pulled her into his arms. "I don't know what I did to deserve you."

She reached up to tug his head closer. When her lips hovered a breath from his, she said, "You did everything right."

With a growl of joy and pleasure, he kissed her, sealing their future together.

* * * * *

Look for BODY OF EVIDENCE
by Lenora Worth,
the next book in the exciting
TEXAS RANGER JUSTICE *series,*
coming soon from Love Inspired Suspense.

Dear Reader,

I hope you enjoyed the first book in the TEXAS
RANGER JUSTICE continuity series. Writing
about Texas Rangers was a first for me and I thor-
oughly enjoyed delving into the life of a Ranger.
The Texas Rangers have a long and exciting history that inspires admiration. Thank you for the
opportunity to introduce you to Ranger Ben Fritz
and I hope you are looking forward to getting to
know the other Texas Rangers in this series.

Corinna Pike suffered a terrible tragedy when
she found her beloved father murdered. At first,
angry at God for allowing this to happen, she had
to come to a place where she could once again
trust her Heavenly Father. Balancing Corinna's
grief and her growing feelings for Ranger Ben
Fritz proved challenging but in the end her love
couldn't be denied. Through Ben's steadfast commitment to God, Corinna and justice, he managed
not only to protect her, but to fall in love with her
as well.

Blessings,

QUESTIONS FOR DISCUSSION

1. What made you pick up this book to read? Did it live up to your expectations? How so?

2. In what ways were Ben and Corinna realistic characters? How did their romance build believably?

3. Talk about the secondary characters. What did you like or dislike about the people in the story?

4. Was the setting clear and appealing? Could you "see" where the story took place?

5. Corinna was angry that God didn't answer her prayers for her father's protection. Have you experienced times where God's answer to your prayers wasn't the answer you sought? Explain.

6. Ben told Corinna evil had killed her father. What does this statement mean to you?

7. Why do you think God allows free will?

8.   Corinna revealed that she danced because it was her mother's wish for her life. What are some expectations that have been placed on you? How did you deal with them?

9.   Though the Miriam Shelter is fictional, the issue of domestic violence is very real. In what ways could you help those suffering from this issue in your community?

10. Corinna found value in volunteering her talent to teach the children of the shelter to dance. Can you share about the talents God gave you? In what ways are you using those talents for good?

11. The loss of her father affected Corinna deeply. Can you share a loss that had touched your life? How did it change you?

12. Ben took his promise to watch over Corinna seriously. Can you share a promise you've made that was important for you to keep?

13. Did you notice the Scripture in the beginning of the book? What do you think these words mean? What application does it have to your life?

14. How did the author's use of language/writing style make this an enjoyable read? Would you read more from this author? If so, why? Or why not?

15. What will be your most vivid memories of this book? What lessons about life, love and faith did you learn from this story?

LARGER-PRINT BOOKS!

GET 2 FREE
LARGER-PRINT NOVELS
PLUS 2 FREE
MYSTERY GIFTS

Love Inspired
SUSPENSE
RIVETING INSPIRATIONAL ROMANCE

Larger-print novels are now available...

YES! Please send me 2 FREE LARGER-PRINT Love Inspired® Suspense novels and my 2 FREE mystery gifts (gifts are worth about $10). After receiving them, if I don't wish to receive any more books, I can return the shipping statement marked "cancel". If I don't cancel, I will receive 4 brand-new novels every month and be billed just $4.74 per book in the U.S. or $5.24 per book in Canada. That's a saving of over 20% off the cover price. It's quite a bargain! Shipping and handling is just 50¢ per book.* I understand that accepting the 2 free books and gifts places me under no obligation to buy anything. I can always return a shipment and cancel at any time. Even if I never buy another book, the two free books and gifts are mine to keep forever.

110/310 IDN E7RD

Name _____ (PLEASE PRINT) _____

Address _____ Apt. # _____

City _____ State/Prov. _____ Zip/Postal Code _____

Signature (if under 18, a parent or guardian must sign)

Mail to **Steeple Hill Reader Service:**
IN U.S.A.: P.O. Box 1867, Buffalo, NY 14240-1867
IN CANADA: P.O. Box 609, Fort Erie, Ontario L2A 5X3

Not valid for current subscribers to Love Inspired Suspense larger-print books.

**Are you a current subscriber to Love Inspired Suspense books
and want to receive the larger-print edition?
Call 1-800-873-8635 or visit www.morefreebooks.com.**

* Terms and prices subject to change without notice. Prices do not include applicable taxes. Sales tax applicable in N.Y. Canadian residents will be charged applicable provincial taxes and GST. Offer not valid in Quebec. This offer is limited to one order per household. All orders subject to approval. Credit or debit balances in a customer's account(s) may be offset by any other outstanding balance owed by or to the customer. Please allow 4 to 6 weeks for delivery. Offer available while quantities last.

Your Privacy: Steeple Hill Books is committed to protecting your privacy. Our Privacy Policy is available online at www.SteepleHill.com or upon request from the Reader Service. From time to time we make our lists of customers available to reputable third parties who may have a product or service of interest to you. If you would prefer we not share your name and address, please check here. ☐

Help us get it right—We strive for accurate, respectful and relevant communications. To clarify or modify your communication preferences, visit us at www.ReaderService.com/consumerchoice.

LISUSLP10R

LARGER-PRINT BOOKS!

**GET 2 FREE
LARGER-PRINT NOVELS
PLUS 2 FREE
MYSTERY GIFTS**

Larger-print novels are now available...

LILP10R